Behutet: The Warrior Within

A novel

The Kamitic legend of Heru of Behutet (Herukhuti) – who symbolizes the ultimate victory over evil – existed before, and served as the model for, such Greek warrior heroes as Hercules, Ares, Jason etc.

Behutet is an urban Kamitic legends genre – a true blend of the ancient with the present where dynamic characters transcend time. *Behutet* has skillfully created a new genre integrating Kamitic cosmology into contemporary lifestyle.

A long awaited book! A must-read!

Book cover designed by Enensa Amen of Graphika Group

Second Printing, February 2012
First Printing 2011
Library of Congress Cataloging-in-Publication Data
p. cm.

Kazembe Bediako: Behutet: The Warrior Within – 1st ed. (Soft Cover)
ISBN 978-0-9845715-0-5   0-9845715-0-7
    1. Mythology. 2. Historical Fantasy Fiction.
    3. Africana Studies. 4. Martial Arts. 5. Spirituality.
    6. Pan African Studies 7. Gender Studies. 8. Urban Kamitic Legends.
    Fiction 1 Title
    Library of Congress Catalog Card Number: 2010906864

Also by
Kazembe Bediako
aka Shekhem Meter Unnerta

Behutet: The Defeat of the Sebau
The second book in the *Behutet* trilogy

Coming Soon

*Leaves of Life: Select Medicinal Plants of Guyana with Healing
Properties*
Volume 1: Single Herbs

Behutet: The Destruction of Man
The third and final book in the *Behutet* trilogy

Read selections from these texts by visiting
www.kazembebediako.com

Khianga Publishing

Dedication

To my mother, Mrs. Inez Hodge and to my father, the late Mr. Wilfred O. Hodge.

Acknowledgements

I would like to thank my mother, Mrs. Inez Hodge, my father, the late Mr. Wilfred O. Hodge, and my grandmother, the late Mrs. Alberta Harding, for making this book possible. My children, Amkhetnu, Basta Maat, Khat Sa Ra and Autqem Neter deserve special thanks for watching over my shoulder as I worked. Special thanks to the editors, Ausura Senuas, Monique Guillory, Auset En Aungkh, Shekhemt Maauti Urrama and Hrimgala Maati Khum for their questions, comments and suggestions.

My wonderful wife Ausara deserves special thanks for letting me work on the computer at all hours of night while writing this book. She was also instrumental in making sure that everything came together at the proper time.

Last, but not least, I thank my spiritual teacher, Shekhem Ur Shekhem, Ra Unnefer Amen I, for reminding us of the greatness of ourselves and our culture. *Anetch Hrak*!

Second Printing

Thank you Shekhemt Nu Aumu for proofreading the book for the second printing and for your editorial suggestions.

Anetch Hrauten Urt Auat EnenTchaas Ra Enkamit and her Sheps, RoshamanaMaa, who brought forth the male virility mudram and inspired the writing of *Behutet*.

TABLE OF CONTENTS

PREFACE

Before Hercules (Heracles), Ares and other Greek warrior heroes, there existed the Kamitic (Ancient Egyptian) legends of Heru of Behutet, or Herukhuti.

According to Herodotus of Halicarnassus, an ancient Greek historian who lived in the 5th century B.C. (c. 484 B.C.– c. 425 B.C.) and is regarded as the 'father of (Western) history,' the Greeks copied the Kamitic religious symbols and adopted their dieties without acknowledging the Egyptian sources. In Book II of his *Histories,* Herodotus argues, "the Egyptians did not take the name of Heracles from the Hellenes (Greeks), but rather the Hellenes from the Egyptians. "[1] During his lengthy travels in ancient Egypt, he was able to observe the history, geography and customs. Herodotus admitted, "besides many other evidences there is chiefly this, namely that the parents of this Heracles, Amphitryon and Alcmene, were both of Egypt."[2] In regard to the antiquity of the names, Herodotus claimed, "In fact however Heracles is a very ancient Egyptian God; and (as they say themselves) it is seventeen thousand years to the beginning of the reign of Amasis from the time when the twelve

---

[1] Herodotus. "Being The Second Book of His Histories Called Euterpe." Trans. G. C. Macaulay. *An Account of Egypt.* Project Gutenberg, 26 Feb. 2006. Web. <http://www.gutenberg.org/2/1/3/2131/>; 9.
[2] Ibid., 9.

gods, of whom they count that Heracles is one, were begotten of the eight gods."[3]

In regard to Greek plagiarism, Herodotus further claims, "the Greeks, however (those I mean who gave the son of Amphitryon that name), took the name from the Egyptians, and not the Egyptians from the Greeks, is I think clearly proved, among other arguments, by the fact that both the parents of Hercules, Amphitryon as well as Alcmena, were of Egyptian origin."[4]

Dr. G.M. James, author of *Stolen Legacy: The Greeks Were Not the Authors of Greek Philosophy, But the People of North Africa, Commonly Called the Egyptians*, also condemns this blatant act of plagiarism. Dr. James notes, "We can at once see how easy it was for an ambitious and even envious nation to claim a body of unwritten knowledge which would make them great in the eyes of the primitive world."[5] He unmasks the academic deceit in his 1954 publication:

> "The absurdity however, is easily recognized when we remember that the Greek language was used to translate several systems of teachings which the Greeks could not succeed in claiming. Such were the translation of Hebrew Scriptures into Greek, called the Septuagint; and the

[3] Ibid., 9.
[4] Ibid., 8.
[5] James, George G. M. *Stolen Legacy: the Greeks Were Not the Authors of Greek Philosophy, but the People of North Africa, Commonly Called the Egyptians.* New York: Philosophical Library, 1954; 9.

translation of the Christian Gospels, Acts and the Epistles in Greek, still called the Greek New Testament. It is only the unwritten philosophy of the Egyptians translated into Greek that has met with such an unhappy fate: a legacy stolen by the Greeks."[6]

Dr. James served as Professor of Logic and Greek at Livingston College in Salisbury, North Carolina and eventually taught at the University of Arkansas, Pine Bluff.

Ra Un Nefer Amen 1, perhaps the first to decipher the ancient Egyptian Ausarian and Ra spiritual initiation systems, decodes the reason for such plagiarism. In his ground breaking *Meter Neter Vol. 1: The Great Oracle of Tehuti and the Egyptian System of Spiritual Cultivation*, he explains:

"Now we can understand why, for example, all the fundamental skills and institutions of civilization began with Black nations (Kamit [Ancient Egypt], Sumer, Babylon, Elam, the Harappa Valley civilization, Kush [Ethiopia], Indus Kush [Black India], and Canaan). Because of their people's ability to learn from the internal part of being, with its storehouse of knowledge concerning every secret of the world, they were able to intuit, 6000+ years ago, the knowledge that forms the basis of our civilization (religion, sculpturing, algebra,

---

[6] Ibid., 9.

science, etc.). Because Western man is polarized in the cultivation of the external part of his being, he had to learn these skills from others (Blacks and Orientals) who were able to learn these things intuitively."[7]

E. A. Wallis Budge, a prolific author of numerous hieroglyphic translations and publications on Egyptian religion argues that the religion of Osiris (Ausar) emerged from an indigenous African people, and he discredits any Greek authenticity regarding the origins of these deities. In the preface to *The Gods of the Egyptians, Vol.1,* Budge concludes that the Greeks were incapable of understanding the cosmogony they copied from the Egyptians:

> "The only beliefs of the Egyptian religion which the educated Greek or Roman truly understood were those which characterized the various forms of Aryan religion, namely, the polytheistic and the solar; for the forms of the cults of the dead, and for all the religious ceremonies and observances, which presupposed a belief in the resurrection of the dead and in everlasting life, and which had been in existence among the indigenous inhabitants of north-east Africa from predynastic times, he had no

---

[7] Amen 1, Ra Un Nefer. *Metu Neter Vol. 1: The Great Oracle of Tehuti and the Egyptian System of Spiritual Cultivation.* Bronx, NY: Khamit Corp., 1990; 7-8.

regard whatsoever. The evidence on the subject now available indicates that he [the Greeks] was racially incapable of appreciating the importance of such beliefs to those who held them, and that although, as in the case of the Ptolomies, he was ready to tolerate, and even, for state purposes, to adopt them, It was impossible for him to absorb them into his life."[8]

Budge career at the British Museum is extensive. He was Keeper of the Egyptian and Assyrian Antiquities at the British Museum from 1894-1924 specializing in Egyptology.

Ra Un Nefer Amen 1 explains why the Greeks copied so extensively from the ancient Egyptians:

"During the first 2000 years of history (4000–2000 B.C.) the only nations that attained to a high degree of civilization were Kamit (Ancient Egypt), Sumer, Babylon, Canaan, Harappa Valley, and Kush (Ethiopia). Although it is well known to all serious historians that all these nations were Black, to this day much effort is being made to hide the fact the fact from the general population. With some it is due to racism. With others it is due to feelings of shame over the fact that throughout the first 4000 years of history (6000 B.C.) it is well known that

---

[8] Budge, E. A. Wallis. *The Gods of the Egyptians: or Studies in Egyptian Mythology, Vol.1.* Chicago: The Open Court Publishing House, 1904: *VIII.*

Preface

Western people had attained to very little cultural
development as well as the fact that they are indebted to
the above Black nations for the foundation of their
scientific, religious, and philosophical
accomplishments."[9]

The inspiration for the main character in the *Behutet* trilogy,
Ra Heru Khuti, was the Kamitic diety Herukhuti also known as
the *Dweller in Behutet, Heru of the Double Splender* or *Light
and Heru of the Doubled Fire.*[10] There have been many, though
arguably faulty, translations of Herukhuti throughout history. As
previously shown, the Kamitic Herukhuti appears as Hercules in
Greek Mythology (*The Histories of Herodotus*, Book II, c.440
B.C.E.).

The story of the *"Legend of Heru-Behutet and the Winged
Disk,"* printed in hieroglyphics and illustrated by large bas-relief
on the walls of the Temple of Edfu in Upper Egypt, and was
translated by Budge in *Legends of the Gods,* features Herukhuti
as Ra Harmakhis.[11] Budge once again amplifies the Kamitic
deity Herukhuti in *The Gods of the Egyptians.* In so doing,
Budge provides the English translation for the story of Heru of

[9] Amen 1, Ra Un Nefer 1990: See page 14.
[10] Amen 1, Ra Un Nefer. *Meter Neter Vol 2: Anuk Ausar, the Kamitc Initation System.* Brooklyn, NY: Khamit Media Trans Visions, Inc., 1994; 77.
[11] Budge, Wallace E. A. *Legends of the Gods.* Project Gutenberg. Dec. 2005. <http://www.gutenberg.org/ebooks/9411>; 16.

Behutet that was carved in hieroglyphics in the temple of Edfu in Upper Egypt.

Other variations of the story Horus (Heru of Edfu) and the Winged Disks were written in French and German. Budge tells us, in 1870 Professor Naville published *Mythe d'Horus*, followed by Heinrich Karl Brugsch in the *Ahandlungen der GottingeAkademie*,[12] and another by Albert Wiedemann in *Die Religion Der Alten Ägypter.*[13]

These translations of the hieroglyphics on the temple of Heru of Edfu incorrectly tell of the conquest of Egypt by an early king (Herukhuti) and his son (Heru Behutet) who, having subdued the peoples in the South, advanced northwards, and made all the people whom he conquered submit to his rule. Budge is guilty of the very charge he laid against the unknown writer who recorded the legend. He criticizes, "the writer of the legend as we have it was not well acquainted with Egyptian history, and that in his account of the conquest of Egypt he has confounded one god with another, and mixed up historical facts with mythological legends to such a degree that his meaning is frequently uncertain."[14]

---

[12] Ibid., 16.

[13] Ibid., 16; also Wiedemann, Albert. *Die Religion Der Alten Ägypter.* Germany: Münster i. W., Aschendorff, 1890. (Harvard University collections): p. 38 ff.

[14] Budge, Wallace E. A. *Legends of the Gods.* Project Gutenberg. Dec. 2005. <http://www.gutenberg.org/ebooks/9411>; 16.

Preface

In *The Gods of the Egyptians*, Herukhuti is called "Horus of the two horizons," or the Harmachis of the Greeks. In the same text, Budge reveals, "The largest known monument or figure of Heru-khuti is the famous Sphinx, near the Pyramids of Gizeh."[15]

In Kamitic cosmology, Herukhuti appears in many forms including having the head of a hawk, wearing the solar disk encircled with two cobras projecting from each lower side, symbolizing the protector of the divine order, Maat which Ra depended on for his existence and work of creator and sustainer of the world.[16] The two cobras are his two great psychic weapons conceptualized as the fire spitting cobra goddesses Nekhebet and Uatchet. His method is brute force. When Herukhuti appears as Heru of Behutet, this is one of the most important forms for "it was under this form that Heru waged war against Set or (The Greek) Typhon, and the inscriptions are full of allusions to the glorious victory which the god of light gained over the prince of darkness and his fiends."[17] This passage is alluding to the battle that took place between Heru and Set whereby Heru castrated Set and Set injured one of Heru's eyes.

This is the empty and mundane form of Herukhuti that most of the Greek mythical figures such as Jason of the Argonauts, the

---

[15] Budge 1904: see page 472.
[16] Amen 1, Ra Un Nefer. *Meter Neter Vol 2: Anuk Ausar, the Kamitic Initiation System.* Brooklyn, NY: Khamit Media Trans Visions, Inc., 1994; 77.
[17] Ibid., 472.

adventures of Hercules, the battles of Ares etc. follow. They all explore the left-brain stories that appeal to the emotions and intellect while in reality they are allegorical.

In its correct form the allegorical story refers to one of the oldest initiation systems in the kamitic cosmological system involving the diety Herukhuti. Behutet (as will be explained later in detail is the form in which Heru fights against Set in order to regain control over of his throne which Set seized) is an aspect of this faculty. The ancient Egyptians protected their inner religious initiation systems from outsiders (foreigners) by creating a (a) "secret order [whereby] membership was gained by initiation and a pledge to secrecy,"[18] and (b) by hiding them in stories that only the initiate would readily identify but would be lost to the outsider. Take, for example, the characteristics of Herukhuti in the spiritual teachings of the Ancient Egyptians.

In the Kamitic tradition Heru of Behutet is an aspect of Herukhuti,[19] the divine principle of justice and protection from suffering.[20] In this form Heru fights Set to regain control of his throne (life). Ra Un Nefer Amen 1 lists the characeristics of Herukhuti in the *Metu Neter Vol 1*. In the Canaanite tradition,

---

[18] James, George G. M. *Stolen Legacy: the Greeks Were Not the Authors of Greek Philosophy, but the People of North Africa, Commonly Called the Egyptians.* New York: Philosophical Library, 1954; 7.
[19] Amen 1, Ra Un Nefer. *Maat: The 11 Laws of God.* Brooklyn, NY: Khamit Publications, Inc., 2003; See page 96.
[20] Ibid., 95.

which evolved from the Kamitic traidition, and from which Judaism borrowed much of their cosmogony, Herukhuti is called Khama-El. In the Kabalistic tradition, he is called Geburah. In the Yoruba tradition, he is called Ogun and Bagalamukhi in the Black tradition of Indus Kush. His energy is governed by the planet Mars, he is assigned the day of Tuesday, his color is blood red and purple and his number is eleven (11).[21] In images, Herukhuti is depicted as a hawk headed or lion headed man carrying a spear with a head of iron in one hand, and an iron chain in the other. In other versions of the Kamitic tradition, the deity carries holds a cutlass or a spear. When you look at the image of the deity, you find that the deity deals with dangerous situations. He deals with killing, defense, offense, force, warriors, police, the military, conflict, zeal, swift action, courage, arrogance, high energy, seizing the moment, and his most celebrated deed was the defeat in battle of Set--the archetype of evil- and his confederate.

According to the Ausarian Initiation system, the Law of Herukhuti is to *"nurture peace and oneness with all through the impersonal mechanism of cause and effect."* [22] God does not punish nor and does he protect. Protection comes from the

---

[21] Amen 1, Ra Un Nefer. *Meter Neter Vol 1: The Great Oracle of Tehuti and the Egyptian System of Spiritual Cultivation.* Brooklyn, NY: Khamit, 1990; 280.

[22] Amen 1, Ra Un Nefer. *Meter Neter Vol 4: The Initiates Daily Meditaion Guide.* Brooklyn, NY: Khamit Media Trans Visions, Inc., 2010; 177.

realization of one's divinity. We are destined to experience challenges/difficulties in life in order to realize the peace that flows from such challenges. Adversity yields wisdom and power. We experience the influence of the Neter Herukhuti as the desire for guaranteed security and protection. This desire can only be satisfied through Herukhuti's Law of Justice.

The law of Herukhuti is to nurture peace and oneness with all through the impersonal mechanism of cause and effect. All events in the world are governed by the law of cause and effect. If you sow good will and love to others, even if they commit injustice towards you, you will eventually reap good will and love. If you sow ill will to others, even as a self-defensive (vengeance, etc.), you will reap ill will from others.

The narrative that is inscribed on the walls of the temple of Edfu,

depicts Heru-Behutet as the "god of light [as] he fought against Set, the god of darkness, and as the god of good against the god of evil. We know from a passage in the xviith Chapter of *the Book of the Dead* (line 66) that in very early times a combat took place between Horus (Heru) and Set, wherein the former destroyed the virility of Set, and the latter cast filth in the face of Horus (Heru). This story is the traditional fight between the two "Combatants," or Rehui."[23]

---

[23] Budge 1904; see page 475.

Preface

When Ra Heru Khuti (in the form of Heru Behutet) battles Sethe is clear headed because there is no feeling of emotional and sensual antagonism within him as there is with Set. There is no mental confusion or doubts about his ability to succeed. This is the sign that he has achieved the state of *Heru Behutet, the ability* to *defeat evil within his being.*

Ra Un Nefer Amen 1 writes about this ancient Egyptian ritual, "You are master of the earth through your likeness with God and go forth to confront the challenging situations in your life. Initiate the situations that need to be confronted. These rituals of confrontation are called Heru Behutet Rituals."[24]

Ra Heru Khuti successfully confronts his fears and anger that arise when he is face to face with Sethe who killed his mentor Shekhem Kesnu Neter and many others in search of the *Papyrus Am Tuat.* Sethe is the cause of the destruction and problems in his life. He meets Sethe with the conviction that his sword is forged in the fires of Amen (peace) and he is at peace in every situation because he followed the counsel of the divine Oracle of Tehuti (the word of God) and the psychic powers of Uatchet and Nehkebet. Finally, in the end, Ra Heru Khuti discovered the *Warrior Within* by defeating evil within his being and became a devine warrior for peace and justice in the world.

---

[24] Amen 1, Ra Un Nefer. *Meter Neter Vol 4 The Initiates Daily Meditaton Guide.* Brooklyn, NY: Khamit Media Trans Visions, Inc., 2010; 249.

Chapter 1: Mount Behutet

The sun rose and blazed sharply against the jagged mountain of rusted iron. Ra Heru Khuti stood at the base of the mountain. At his feet lay his chains and spear he used to capture and subdue his enemies. His white t-shirt and loose linen pants matted against his dark sweaty body. Like his father before him, he now sat in semi-dhummo, his hands firmly placed on the ground in the shape of a pyramid, contemplating the monstrous *Mount Behutet* which had claimed the lives of so many. He could smell the acid blood on the rusted teeth and spires of the mountain.

There was no clear path up the mountain. Sethe had covered his tracks well and had altered his appearance. Ra Heru Khuti did not know what form he had taken. He heard the strange hissing sounds from among the sharp rocks and knew Sethe had changed into the form of a serpent. He now relied on his uncle's spirit, Heru Ur, to guide him to find the most accessible path to the top. He chose the north face of *Mount Behutet*. Even though this was considered the most dangerous path, his guides *Nekhebet* and *Uatchet* insisted this was Sethe's only escape route. Clouds hung in a light blue sky. Ra Heru Khuti gazed up at the sky watching the clouds move, revealing a clear endless brilliance. He fixed his inner eyes on the task ahead. Behind him, the younger boys, whose time would soon come to perform this ritual, stood in awe, their fingers restlessly tapping on their *Djembes, Lambes and Djuns Djuns* as they awaited a signal from the Ser-u.

Today, the elders, also called the Ser-u and Sert-u, walked with an air of authority about them, their robes hung stubbornly on their shoulders. The young drummers inhaled the warm fresh air as the brisk summer breeze whispered across their sweaty faces. Ra Heru Khuti stood in unison with everything around him. *Mount Behutet* beckoned. Yet, to the crowd that gathered to witness this annual feat, he appeared undisturbed by the green grass and tall bushes that opened the way for him. The smell of frankincense and pine trees filled his nostrils. He climbed through the sharp stony winding path crushing the rocks with his bare feet. He mounted the path's twists and turns effortlessly, his mind focused on slaughtering the enemies of Ausar, his father. The sun glowed and glowed but Ra Heru Khuti's only concern was to reach the top.

"Must I climb this mountain too?" the little boy asked the Sheps Rashamana Maat, the honorable and elderly woman standing next to him at the base of the mountain. It was through her that the Ritual of Overthrowing Sethe and being accepted into the Shemsu Heru came into being so many years ago.

"You will climb this mountain and many more inside of you!" she answered mysteriously. "You will have many lives of climbing to be accepted into the Shemsu Heru," she added as she blended into the sea of white dresses worn by the female devotees.

As Ra Heru Khuti climbed, there was no sense of sluggishness, or fatigue. He glanced at the fierce hippopotamus and the crocodiles lazing on the other side of the mountain curious at his brazen presence before them. They took to snapping haplessly at his feet and when they were near enough to him, they opened their mouths as though he might just walk right in. But the gaping jaws of the crocodiles appeared to salute Ra Heru Khuti as he charged forth on his mission to destroy the rebel Sethe who had terrorized the countryside with his wicked band of confederates.

The jagged mountain top was finally in view but before he could take the summit, a large boulder blocked his path. The terrible Merti snake, one of a group of venomous serpents that live by slaughtering those who dare to climb *Mount Behutet,* sat on top of the boulder. Like the sun and the jagged rocks, the hippo and the toothy crocodile, this obstacle did not faze him and he stepped upon it as though he might simply walk through it. But within the first two steps, the boulder shifted and flopped towards him in a dense and brutal roll, driving to crush him. The

Serpent coiled itself around the boulder hissing deadly venom. There was no break, no relief on this path lined with sharp rocks and crags, hot as a new blade fresh from the fire. He drew his spear forged by the blacksmith friends in Edfu in the blaze of Amen, and struck the boulder in its center as the non-legged beast descended upon him. The boulder, along with the venomous Merti serpent, instantly exploded into many pieces that shot off in different directions, revealing a vast plateau before him.

Ra Heru Khuti gazed out over the mountain and the valley below him and discovered a field of pine and holly trees. He rushed through the field and came upon a cave which, upon closer inspection, appeared to be a temple. Within a few feet of its opening, no natural light could make its way into the cave but it seemed to glow and radiate with a brilliance that drew Ra Heru Khuti deeper inside. He soon saw that the cave was illuminated from within, from a remote crevasse where the eternal sun triumphed and conquered the cave's darkness. Tiny particles danced in the beam of light and showered an air of divine tranquility upon Sethe who sat in a deep meditative state. Ra Heru Khuti stood in awe gazing upon Sethe, who reminded him of his forefathers when they sat in an alabaster chair during the solstice ritual receiving the wisdom of the stars.

Sethe's body swayed lightly and he was so deeply possessed that hat he did not hear Ra Heru Khuti enter his chamber in the cave. The two men faced each other squarely – one blindly possessed with the rage for dominance, the other ablaze with the fire of justice and on guard for the battle that would ensue. When Sethe finally opened his eyes, he was greatly vexed upon recognizing Ra Heru Khuti standing in front of him. Without a word, he nodded his head to the recesses of the cave and two hulking men dressed in pristine white robes emerged. The guards, Apep and Ap, entered the chamber of evil as Sethe manipulated the magical sequence to command his followers. Sethe sat with a silver sword in the eastern direction, a long wooden wand lay in the southern tip of the star, while a bowl of sea water lay in the north and gold coins in the west. On the ground around them were strange line drawings which pulsated with energy. In fact they had a glow about them that rendered the room rather luminescent. Sethe's eyes were still rolled back into his head as he tried in vain to contain himself. Suddenly he began to float up into the air as a sickening glow overwhelmed his pallid skin.

"Ahhh! The Magical *Papyrus Am Tuat*! ..." he gasped in the voice of a wise old man. The elder of his two guards dressed in white robes gasped as well.

"That voice I recognize it!" Ra Heru Khuti pondered for a moment. "Great gods! It is his grandfather Mortimer Sethe's voice!"

"Yes, it is good to see that you recognize me, for time is against us. We must find and stand on the magical *Papyrus Am Tuat*, as it will transform us from our limited heavy leaden states into our infinite potential as rulers of the world! Only then will we be able to enslave the earth. We must wrest it from the grasp of the Shemsu Heru before their filthy hands defile it. We must do this for our beloved fraternity of the night, even if it means we must devour them!" And, with that, Sethe collapsed upon the ground.

Sethe awoke to find he was lying at the foot of Ra Heru Khuti. "Where am I?" he murmured in bewilderment. "Wait. Is this not the place, where the temple of my grandfather was burned to the ground?" On seeing Ra Heru Khuti he uttered two magical words of a spell and disappeared. Ra Heru Khuti quickly gave chase while chanting the words of power given to him by his uncle Heru Ur and then teleporting himself towards Sethe.

"Hey what are you doing here?" Sethe changed the tone of his voice to a gruff one as he attempted to grab the *Papyrus Am Tuat* from Ra Heru Khuti's hands.

Ra Heru Khuti deflected the movement with a chanted word, *"Phat!"* The *Papyrus Am Tuat* smacked against Sethe's head and

Ra Heru Khuti buckled to his knees. "What happened? That word usually works," Ra Heru Khuti mused.

Sethe noticed the *Papyrus Am Tuat* in the young man's hands. "Where did you get the *Papyrus Am Tuat*? It belongs to us!" Sethe snarled.

"Belongs to whom? For 3,000 years this *Papyrus Am Tuat*'s been under the protection of the Shemsu Heru. How does that make it yours?" Ra Heru Khuti challenged. With that, he tucked the *Papyrus Am Tuat* under his arm and in one sweeping motion summoned the sun's rays into a ball. Sethe and his two henchmen, Apep and Ap, surrounded him, sweat dripping off their bodies. The ball of rays in his hand reflected red rubies, garnets, and sapphires. As Ra Heru Khuti prepared to hurl the ball at Sethe, suddenly, out of nowhere, appeared a large golden sphere with a feather engraved upon it. A large, golden goblet stood in the midst of the sphere. Seeing the feather floating in the air and knowing that the goddess Maat was about to make her entrance, Sethe's henchmen, Apep and Ap fled the temple in fear. Their screams wailed across the sky as they hurled themselves from the mountain top, landing between the jagged rocks of the mountain ridges. But Sethe was not moved so easily. He vanished into thin air.

At the bottom of the mountain in a moment of unrehearsed unison the crowd's thunderous voices shattered the screams of

Sethe's henchmen and rang out, *"Asheyon..."* They chanted to Heru as their fathers before them had chanted and their fathers before them who were abducted onto boats and sailed into the Tuat, and their fathers before them in the savannas of the Congo before they sailed up the Nile to Punt and Kush, Nubia and Khamit...They chanted as the ancients did for the first time at the base of the magical mountain of the moon in *Bambalasam*.

"Asheyon...." They chose to offer Heru a permanent place within their beings. Their voices boomed, shattering the walls of the temple cave, sending a burst of energy over the fields, down to the valley where the *Djembes, Lambes and Djuns Djuns* answered them in fiery rhythms. The young children possessed by this energy tumbled cartwheels, flipping and contorting their bodies around each other in the hot sand. The old women danced nimbly with smiles on their smooth faces as the voices of their young men filled the land. Even the clouds halted their eternal journey and held tight the azure sky. They listened to the voices of their young men choosing to accept Heru permanently in their spirits. The hawk headed young men drank from the golden goblet that passed through the ages as a symbol of their vitality, and the freedom to choose to be god men while traveling in the Tuat.

Ra Heru Khuti straddled the jagged mountaintop, the divine spear in one hand and the *Papyrus Am Tuat* in the other. The mountain seemed to be erupting in volcanic red lava as the hawk headed young men at the base of the mountain drank from the goblet, renewing the rays of life swelling inside of them – emanating through them, knowing one day, they too would climb the mountain to *Behutet*, a mountain they would climb a thousand times, if need be, in their lives. It was then that Un-Nefer, lord of the Herukhuti shrine, stood up. All faces were upon him as he strode over to the young men. The *Urrt Crown* sat upon his head offering protection to all those who dwell in the peace of Amen. A brilliant light shone upon his face and embraced all who surrounded him. "The *Mesu Betshet* will rise no more!" Un-Nefer reassured every one as he started his climb to *Mount Behutet*.

Chapter 2: Ancestral Dance

Ra Heru Khuti nervously tiptoed his way out of the bathroom and into the bedroom, softly singing "*Asheyon. Asheyon.*" He stood beside the bed, dripping wet, gazing down on the prostrated figure on the bed. Mehurt lay cuddled within the sheets wrapped around her waist. He still held the wet towel poised in his hands. The tension in his face and body reflected the impending scene that was to follow. As he leaned closer to her, he felt her warm breath against his arm. He began to doubt himself. What seemed so simple and clear in his mind now created hesitation and doubt.

He felt a curious itch in the back of his neck as if someone was watching him, as if someone else was in the room. His hands reached out further for her neck. The wind blew the curtains aside and a beam of light from the street lamp broke into the room, illuminating his naked body. Mehurt always made fun of his bashfulness when it came to his nakedness. She was quite the opposite. Rarely would she go about her house fully dressed. To her, clothing was symbolic. She equated clothing with pretences and took advantage of every opportunity to rid herself of the pretences that clouded her life. He always thought it funny when she used the bathroom and took off all her clothing just to urinate. She claimed it made her feel less restricted and her urine flowed freely and unimpeded.

As the beam of light hugged his naked body, he shivered with the thought of Mehurt's waking up and discovering him in the act. Streaks of warm perspiration crawled down the side of his cheeks. His breathing became louder. He carefully eased one end of the towel under her neck. As he did so, Mehurt turned in her sleep, and nestled her face in the palm of her hand. He held his breath, hoping she would not wake. But as if sensing his discomfort, she quietly rolled onto her side with her back towards him. Ra Heru Khuti hesitated for a few minutes, passed his right palm in front of her eyes to ensure she was asleep. She was known to have extra sensory powers. Then in a quick sweeping motion with his hands he brought the ends of the towel together tightening it around her waist. Mehurt rustled in her sleep. Her eyes peeped open and a smile covered her face.

"Not now honey!" She chided him. He paused as if in a stupor but her open arms invited him to nestle into them.

As he lay cuddled between her arms, she seemed to cast a spell over him and took his thoughts back to their first meeting. They had met at a party given by Khepri, a mysterious, wealthy ex-banker on a collision course with self destruction. The people in the room that seemed to represent every facet of society intrigued Ra Heru Khuti: from academicians to thieves, prostitutes and housewives, artists, law enforcement, doctors, lawyers, architects, financiers with their investors, and of course, the politicians and clergy. He positioned himself near the grand piano being used as a bar in a corner of the ballroom so he could observe the party goers when Mehurt bumped into him. Mehurt struck him as a bored woman looking for some entertainment in her life. Her hazel brown eyes tantalized him while her lips hung limpid, giving flavor to her words.

"Why de man stare so?" she queried in her Jamaican sing-song accent. His words stumbled and tripped in the back of his throat.

"Cat got ya tongue, uh!" She giggled, flirting with him. She laid her soft brown body against his hands, sliding her lips back and forth against the rim of her glass.

"I wasn't staring. I was looking for someone!" He lied.

"Who ya look fo'?" She mused, curling a piece of ice with her tongue. He gave her his undivided attention when Khepri grabbed her arm and whisked her away. Relieved, he took no exception to her being dragged off. But shortly after, she returned. She wore a long green costume trimmed with gold and a head wrap that covered her forehead and accentuated her hazel eyes. Ra Heru Khuti thought she had the commanding presence of a Queen Mother and he blurted out something to the effect that she looked like Netert without even seeing a portrait of the great Queen Mother Netert.

"Wow! I look like an African Queen!" She boasted.

"Khepri, Khepri, come hear this!" she cried chasing after Khepri. This infuriated Khepri who confronted Ra Heru Khuti.

"Looka here brother. Don't put that stupid talk in her head." But Mehurt was touched. Her eyes darted mischievously back and forth between Ra Heru Khuti and Khepri. She enjoyed the play between the two men. Finally, Mehurt positioned herself between the two men. "Have you two boys met?" Ra Heru Khuti extended his hands toward Khepri who did not reciprocate but instead Khepri strolled off leaving Ra Heru Khuti hanging.

She scolded him again as she lay cuddled in his arms, "This is not an African dance! It is a mudram!"

She performed her movements with ease and fluidity. She was fun to watch. She seemed to make the most difficult movements so easy and graceful. "Most people think I dance but I don't! The ancestors, they create these movements through me!" He watched in astonishment as she rolled her shoulders up and down as if there were no bones in her body, her fingers grasping at the air and gathering energy which she took into her, rolling in and out. Her breathing was effortless and her eyes stared deep into infinity.

"These movements originated below the Mountain of the Moon! where our ancestors awaken *Dambalah Wedo* and *Aida Wedo* in our spirits!" Her fingers spoke as the drums accompanied her gestures. Ra Heru Khuti felt the cool energy tickling his lower back. Mehurt coiled her body and twisted and swirled as if she was another being. Then she stopped, her eyes rolled back into her forehead, "I shall come again to unearth these powers, 'Is Miya Iye, Sosa Ma Iye!'" She sang collapsing in his arms "Oya Sa Miye!"

Chapter 3: Among the Gullah

Mehurt sat on the beach in St. Helena, South Carolina, soaking in the cool white sands watching a group of Gullah women perform the West African dances that survived in the Tuat. As she watched the women with head wraps and linen white dresses sway from side to side, it seemed time stood still for the young girls who sat among the sweet grass that was being woven into baskets.

Mehurt spoke in the same sing song accent as when she first met Ra Heru Khuti. She explained to him, "my accent is not Jamaican patios but the tongue of the Gullah people of South Carolina. My people are Gullah, descendants of West Africans who were stolen and forcibly sent into the Tuat to work the rice and cotton fields before they were freed. They collectively purchased the land they worked. The Gullahs lived in isolation from Western culture for generations during and after slavery, allowing them to maintain their African culture longer than any other Africans in the Tuat."

The west African dance the Gullah women performed symbolized the struggle to maintain tradition and save the island of St. Helena from being snatched up by greedy conglomerates. The performance was to save the Gullahs or the Geechees from extinction.

Mehurt came to South Carolina to participate in the twenty-year-old Gullah Festival held in Beaufort across the bridge from St. Helena. The festival was aimed at spreading the word of their plight and keeping the Gullah customs alive. St. Helena remains overwhelmingly Gullah and is one of only a handful of the Sea Islands or low country still controlled by the people who worked the land. The Gullahs own sixty percent of the land and control, for the most part, what happens to it.

"You Geechee girl?" Ra Heru Khuti teased her.

"Mus tek cyear a de root fa heal de tree." Mehurt replied.

"Tru dat!" he complimented her.

Her stare accused him of hiding something. Finally, she asked, "And you na?"

"I was born in Guyana. We speak Creole," Ra Heru Khuti told her defensively. "Guyana de same as Jamaica, Belize and Sierra Leone. Ma people Sweetgrass basket weavers, long strip quilters, and fabric artists. Yo people rice and sugar growers. All de same!"

Mehurt was one of the few who were able to trace her ancestry back to Africa – back to the Foulah Nation from the town of

Kianah in the District of Temourah in the Kingdom of Massina, on the Niger River.

Later that year he saw her again in Charleston, South Carolina at the Mojoo Festival. Ra Heru Khuti was surprised to see her at the Mojoo Festival because she had moved to the city of Men Nefer to care for her father who was losing his eyesight. Ra Heru Khuti just finished watching an emotionally packed drama entitled "Ebo Landin" performed in front of the Old Slave Mart on Chalmers Street. The story was about eighteen tribesmen who chose death over servitude on St. Simmons Island. The drama was so powerful that Ra Heru Khuti had torn himself away with tears flowing down his angry cheeks. Mehurt found him sitting on bench in Forte Sumter National Park overlooking the Atlantic Ocean. She was doing research on the Seminole nation and invited him to accompany her to Sullivan Island to visit the place where Osceola died in captivity. Osceola was the defiant young leader of the Seminole people who resisted the Indian emigration. In 1832 some Seminole chiefs signed a treaty that called for them to move to Indian Territory in present-day Oklahoma. Osceola and other young Seminoles opposed the move. In 1835 he declared, "This is the only treaty I will make with the whites!" as he plunged his knife into the treaty he was asked to sign that would move his people from their swamplands in the Southeast to the unoccupied territory west of the

Mississippi. This action precipitated the Second Seminole War — a seven-year game of cat-and-mouse in the Florida swamps against federal troops. Finally, tricked into talking peace, Osceola was captured in 1837 while carrying a white flag of truce and imprisoned in Fort Moultrie, Charleston, South Carolina where he died on January 20, 1838 of malaria.

On Sullivan's island Ra Heru Khuti and Mehurt walked in silence on the white sands underneath the lighthouse, each deeply lodged in his and her own memories. He listened to her white linen dress rustling in the dry wind, each whisper telling him a different story of the Seminole people. It was hot and he could feel the sweat streaking down his arms.

"You and Khepri are two different people, how come you know each other?" Mehurt asked as they descended into the dungeon where Osceola had spent his last days.

The tour guide's voice hummed off the walls of the dungeon. "...Betrayed and tortured he spent his last days chanting to his ancestors who are a small offshoot of the Gullah people who escaped from the rice plantations in South Carolina and Georgia. They built their own settlements on the Florida frontier and fought a series of wars to preserve their freedom. In 1818, General Andrew Jackson led an American army into Florida to claim it for the United States, and war erupted. The Blacks and Indians fought side-by-side in a desperate struggle to stop the

American advance, but they were defeated and driven south into the more remote wilderness of central and southern Florida."

The tour guide continued, "In 1835, the Second Seminole War broke out, and this full-scale guerrilla war lasted for six years. The Black Seminoles waged the fiercest resistance as they feared that capture or surrender meant death or return to slavery..." Inside the tight chamber, the walls were hot and sunlight peeked through tiny holes of the outer side.

"I remembered when we used to sit on Puntrench Dam and put on trial, it seemed like, every politician who ran the country into bankruptcy." Ra Heru Khuti told her.

"We were dry-mouthed youth with empty stomachs rebelling against hunger. Work was scarce and the labor unions led the country in a series of labor strikes that crippled the economy. The public schools were closed and used for union meetings, distribution centers and warehouses. During those days we read any material we could find. It was the only way of knowing what was going on in the rest of the world. So, there we were. We became the tears of our countrymen and women," Ra Heru Khuti recalled. Their steps were loud against the dungeon walls.

"Eventually, the night flies and mosquitoes surrounded us. Then Khepri would make a bonfire and our deliberating voices, drenched in idyllic prose, would argue the possibility of viable Caribbean freedoms against the frenzy of dread masquerading with the stagnation of inertia. Our tempestuous voices would rise and sink with the fire. In the end our avid condemnation of the betrayal of the revolution would be overcome by hunger and sleep. Great friends we were then. 'In this great future no one can afford to forget one's past.' Khepri used to say." Ra Heru Khuti reminisced as he answered Mehurt's question.

"Menacing memorabilia of our lost youth!" Mehurt joked.

"You laugh when I talk this way…as if life has gone astray. But little do you know that all tormented souls must find a peaceful abode. Not until we manage to resolve this conflict between being cool and being fools." Ra Heru Khuti had become distant.

He rambled on. "You see things will forever remain the same; getting up would remain pulling down, smiling would remain a lie, being macho would remain masking low egos. In the end, being you would mean being untrue, you see? We remain torn between these opposites, doomed to irreconcilable differences!"

They came upon a room where water dripped from an overhead crack in the wall. In the distant end of the room a dark shadow lay curled beneath the stairs. Both Ra Heru Khuti and Mehurt exchanged glances suspiciously. She took his hand as they walked down the remaining corridors. To Mehurt, this monstrous ruin reverberated with drunken voices-cryptic laughter veiling shameful tears. She thought she espied glimpses of peeking shadows darting from room to room and felt the haunting madness alive in this ruin. She knew the moon shine faces of rage molded into the walls. She began to identify with the montage of suffering, pregnant in the womb of this crumbling tomb.

"I am scared!" Mehurt finally admitted. "Ah wonder what these rocks would say, if they were to talk… what they would testify? What agony, what joys they would recite." She imagined these shadows as distant runners with the light chasing summer's brutality through timid nights. She knew somewhere in these half deserted rooms a Malcolm's war poem stood *en garde*, somewhere in this scorched dungeon a Martin sermon kept vigil. She could not escape the pressing crowds in this overwhelming loneliness. Osceola's face became a mirror of this muscular delusion sprawled out over this dungeon macabre. Finally, they ascended the stairs leading out of the semi-lit rooms back to the beach. On the beach Ra Heru Khuti felt tired.

"Can we sit awhile?" he asked Mehurt. They both were tired and their bodies sank into the cool sand.

"Look" Ra Heru Khuti said pointing in the distance. "Look!" In the distance the ageless figures drifted solemnly in a parade of torsos. Three young girls slipped past them, their fingers interlocked, their girlish laughter echoing in their ears. They watched the little girls skipping along the sea shore. Ra Heru

Khuti smiled with a sense of familiarity in the way they measured up against the breaking silver waves.

"I need a drink," Mehurt sighed impatiently. She disliked the dread-like tension on the island.

"I have to go!" she demanded moving toward the road. Her hasty walk gradually grew into a jog as she ran toward the road. Ra Heru Khuti was puzzled. She ran like she was being chased.

"Youngbloods, Youngbloods" Ra Heru Khuti heard her mumbling as he ran by her side trying to keep up with her. *Me gwine home. Dem dey duh wait fuh we. Me tell 'um say 'e didn't halluh die. Dem Buchruk dey kill 'im. E didn't halluh die!"*

Chapter 4: Headless Horror

"Wait! Wait!" Ra Heru Khuti shouted after Mehurt as he gave chase. Finally, he stopped to catch his breath. She was running too fast. He sank into the cool sand on the beach. As he lay under the retreating sun, sprinkles of water from the waves misted the air. He felt faint-headed and began to relax. Ra Heru Khuti's mind drifted to that state between being awake and sleep. While he was in that half awake, half asleep state, he saw himself jump up as a female figure approached him. She was surrounded by the setting sun whose radiance gave off a brilliant light. "Can't be. No!" he thought. She walked with grace and her feet never touched the sand. She wore a blue green dress that twirled freely in the air encircling her. Her breasts were full and her hips rolled as she walked. She wore a mysteriously shaped hat on her head. From the distance, it looked like a seat surrounded by cool light. It seemed as if her outstretched arms were like the wings of a vulture surrounding him and protecting him. As she approached him, it was as if she turned the sun into a moon. He found the cool light to be refreshing.

Mehurt's voice cracked as she spoke. "Ra Heru Khuti!" she called, *"What is dat thing doing in ma home?"* He stood there trembling. Mehurt's face loomed more into focus standing in the doorway between the kitchen and the dinning room. Her head wrap hung slack against her cheeks. Her sharp hazel brown eyes scrutinized his face. But he stood there in fear and awe, trembling as urine streamed down his legs into a warm pool at his feet. *"What is dat thing doing in ma home?"* she asked again as if he knew. The tone of her voice jarred at the truth. His tongue began to flutter when he tried to talk. Meaningless words escaped his lips. He felt dizzy as the blood rushed from his head. This was no hallucination. Her silent stare often comforted him through these moments of imagined fear, that the grotesque figure was no figment of his imagination, that the headless horror stalking him was no moonlit delusion. Maybe she, too, visited with the horror that now confronted him.

It began long ago when he was ten years old and was playing with his friends in the backyard. He first saw the huge headless man wandering into their midst. While his friends ran, he froze, stood there screaming until he fainted. His grandmother explained to him that what he saw was no figment of his imagination. The apparition's name was Seb. He actually lived next door to them. He was a tall muscular chunk of a man. He stood six feet nine inches and weighed two hundred-and-seventy-eight pounds. He wore his pride wrapped around his head like a house. He was married to Mut…petite, beautiful and flirtatious. That was Mut. Seb was madly in love with Mut who had all the men going stark crazy over her. Seb was a violent man and would attack anyone he suspected of flirting with Mut. He would then turn and physically abuse Mut.

Story had it that Mut and Shu starting flirting the moment they first laid eyes on each other. Their relationship was so intense Mut did not care if Seb found out or not. She couldn't stand being away from Shu. Seb found out about the relationship and violently attacked Shu who was no match for him. The fight took place at the Hell's Kitchen Junction outside Gullah Jack's Bar & Grill. Seb beat Shu so badly even the police were afraid to intervene. They said Seb had hell in his eyes and thunder in his fist. His punches and kicks were so fierce you could hear Shu's screams all the way over Pleasant's Turn, where Lucius and Old Goat Foot Sam were out back fishing. It took Shu over six months of hospitalization to get over that beating.

Seb was never the same after that. He took to heavy drinking. At nights, he would be seen staggering along Puntrench Road singing about his love for Mut.

It was Saturday night. Gullah Jack's Bar & Grill had just opened. Not too many people were around. Lucius, Old Goat Foot Sam, and Bayie were enjoying a quiet conversation, sitting

on a log at Hell's Kitchen Junction. At first they thought
Madman Pea was chopping wood. But the sound was different.
That was when Neith came running down the street hollering at
the top of her lungs. Bayie, Old Goat Foot Sam and Lucius
jumped up and peeked around the corner to see what was wrong
with Neith. "Murdah! Oh gawd! Murdah!" She screamed. Neith
weighed close to three hundred pounds but she ran, barefoot and
all, like her weight was no problem. Bayie, who used to visit
Neith some nights, seemed more concerned than the others but
still he didn't move. As Neith ran, her dress flew up in the air
and her breasts jiggled from side to side. Lucius and Old Goat
Foot Sam seemed more interested in what Neith was revealing
than her distress. By this time a few heads peeked out from
behind the curtains but no one opened the windows or doors and
came to Neith's aid. "Murdah! A man taking heads! Call de
police! There is a man going 'round taking heads!" she
screamed, flying into Gullah Jack's Bar & Grill. Just then Seb,
bloody from the machete's chops staggered around the bend onto
the junction. Shu, machete in hand was still chopping away at
him. Everyone stood in shock except Shu who was intent on
finishing the job. Seb slowly sank to the ground on one knee.
Shu circled him, sizing him carefully; machete held up high and
with one quick maddening blow swung at his victim's neck.

Seb's head rolled down the street where it came to rest beside the log where stood Lucius, Old Goat Foot Sam, and Bayie.

Chapter 5: Behind the Curtains

Khatrasaim lived in a three bedroom apartment in Crown Heights and was having some problems meeting the rent, so when Neru mentioned he was looking for a place because it had become too crowded with his sister and her children, she grabbed the opportunity and invited him to move in with her. Khatrasaim's family was against it and Aqmeri advised against it. Neru's friends wondered what Khatrasaim, so accomplished, was doing with Neru who claimed to be a graphic artist who designed web pages for artists. Neru always carried around his wireless Imac, Ipod, Blackberry Bold 9700, and T-Mobile Sidekick 010 with him. Khatrasaim said she'd never been happier. She said she was in love. Neru dropped out of high school and got his GED instead. He worked in a record store, deejayed, did some telemarketing, had a baby girl with a former girlfriend and went to jail for two years. When he was released he went to audio recording and production school, switched and went back to school to learn web design and founded his own company, Future Graphics, when he met Khatrasaim. His latest thing was designing concert T-shirts and night club websites or videotaping dance parties and bootlegging DVDs and audio CDs. But all his business enterprises lacked funding.

That's when Khetnu introduced Neru to Sahu. His plan was to work for Sahu for two years and he would have enough money to run his business successfully. But Khatrasaim never knew this side of his business. Khatrasaim felt Neru brought her success. Since meeting him she had landed the hottest job of her career at Blackplanet.com as junior executive for marketing. Now her company offered to send her to Atlanta to head the corporate office in Georgia. She was out celebrating with friends and on her way home she stopped and picked up a special bottle of Chateau De La Roulerie, Rose D'Anjou. She had text messaged and voice mailed Neru, asking him to be home when she arrived. She was going to propose that they form a business partnership. She wanted to get him away from his friends whom she had reservations about. She had corporate skills and credentials and he had artistry. She was also concerned about how legitimate Neru's operations were and had called an old friend who was a business consultant to look over some of the websites Neru claimed he had designed.

"Khatrasaim," she told her, "these people don't necessarily look like the type of people I know you to hang out with. Are you comfortable with that?"

"Yea," Khatrasaim told her, "I have thought about it and this is the man I love. As long as he is not disrespectful to me or the relationship I am good." But Khatrasaim lied. Neru had developed a passion and jealousy over her that was frightening.

One weekend she and Aqmeri took off and went to Atlantic City just to unwind. Ladies night out, they called it. She had left Neru several messages since she could not find him. When she got home that Sunday night Neru was sitting in his car parked outside the apartment building. As she walked toward the front door he jumped out of the car and grabbed her.

"Where you been all weekend?" he demanded. "I know you got someone else. You don't have to lie to me. Tell me you got someone else!" She was scared for she had never seen such anger in him like this.

"Aqmeri and I went to Atlantic City!" She tried to explain, but before she finished her sentence he had smacked her in the mouth. The blow was so powerful she fell to the ground.

"Didn't I tell you to stay away from that witch!" he screamed at her. She felt dazed and confused and struggled to her feet only to be knocked back down.

"I told you not to mess with her! Can't you see she's trying to break us up?" he repeated. "Where she at?" he again screamed at her. This time he had a firm grip on her throat.

"The next time I see you with her I am going to choke the daylight out of you!" he promised as he stormed toward his car and drove off.

She felt some of her neighbors peeking at her from behind their curtains. She felt ashamed and confused. No one had ever put their hands on her before. What if her parents heard of this? Her mouth was bleeding. She picked up her bags and ran into the apartment. The bottle of wine was broken and spilled all over her. Neru had just pulled out of the block when Ras arrived at Neru's apartment on Jefferson Street. Khatrasaim was still on the phone talking to Aqmeri who was screaming at her.

"Call the cops! Call the cops! Don't let him get away with this 'cause he gonna do it again! I am calling your father!" Aqmeri threatened her.

Neru was right, "Aqmeri is a meddling trouble maker," Khatrasaim thought. She begged Aqmeri not to call her parents until she worked it out. It had happened all too suddenly. Before she hung up the phone, she again implored Aqmeri not to call her family.

"I am coming right over." Aqmeri said before hanging up the phone, and before you knew it she was ringing Khatrasaim's intercom buzzer. When the intercom rang Khatrasaim pressed the buzzer, wondering how Aqmeri could have gotten there that fast.

Chapter 6: Searching for His Head

Ra Heru Khuti's head lay on his grandmother's shoulder. She too shared in his midnight horror. "Eber since Seb been roamin' searching for his head...searching for his peace," she told him. "But why he here?" she asked him.

That's when he confessed. He and two other friends had masterminded a plot to rob, a local merchant as the businessman deposited his daily earnings in the Greenpoint Savings Bank at the corner of Eastern Parkway and Utica Avenue in Brooklyn. They were to meet around eleven o'clock at Rob's Fried Chicken. At 11:11 pm, Ra Heru Khuti would follow the merchant while pretending to be next on line to use the outside teller machine. As the merchant stepped up to the machine Ra Heru Khuti would distract him while Rupert attacked from behind, hitting the merchant on the head. They would grab the bag and run down Utica Avenue, cut across Rochester Avenue and dart through the park. They would meet on the other side of Pitkin Avenue. But Ra Heru Khuti fell asleep and did not get up on time.

Rupert and Leroi waited for Ra Heru Khuti at Rob's Fried Chicken. At 11:11 pm they decided to go ahead without Ra Heru Khuti. Leroi was on-line after the merchant pretending to make a deposit. As the merchant reached into his bag for his night deposit, Rupert attempted to distract him and as Leroi stepped in, the merchant who was an undercover New York City police officer pulled his hand out of the bag, which concealed a hand gun. He shot both of them.

His grandmother stood in the hallway between Seb and Ra Heru Khuti, pointing her finger accusingly at Seb, *"Wha is dis t'ing doin' in ma home?"* Ra Heru Khuti fell in fear trembling to his knees in a pool of his own urine.

A woman's voice was screaming at the top of her lungs. It was the voice of Mrs. Farley, Rupert's mother. "Oh gawd! De shot ma son, my only son!" She burst down the door and fell onto the floor. "Oh gawd! De shot my boy!" Ra Heru Khuti walked over to her and tried to grab her arm to support her. "Ra Heru Khuti! Ra Heru Khuti! De shot your best friend!" Mrs. Farley wailed.

There was more screaming outside as Mrs. Green, Leroi's mother broke into the room. She couldn't talk. She was in shock. She held her daughter's hand tightly. Her eyes were blood-shot. "Leroi is dead!" she announced, gasping for breath. Both of the boys' mothers grabbed Ra Heru Khuti as they wailed. They suffocated him in their tight grasp while his grandmother rebuked the spirit of headless Seb. He wanted to yell out to them, to tell them that he had conceived the plan that killed their sons. Through this meager exchange of embrace, he tried to soothe their pain away. He tried to undo the harm with his affection. Yet, he still didn't have the courage to tell them he was the cause of their loneliness. His hugs were telling them it was his way of loving the pain away.

Chapter 7: Papyrus Am Tuat

"They should pay us for all the work we do in this place. America was built on the backs of free black labor…built on our sweat and blood for how long?" Ras insisted. His real name was Raul. In his earlier days he was one of the fixed, fiery, box-speakers on the corner of Lenox Avenue and 125th Street. His trade mark was an 8" x 11" page which was folded four times into a size that fit firmly in his palm where he would keenly scribble notes. He was always calm and emitted energy of peace. Whenever there was a disagreement, it was Ras who sent the warring brothers home in peace. Often he would amuse himself with his co-worker they called, Anpu, who was a staunch uncompromising nationalist. In his forties, Ras sported a semi Afro that was growing thin in the middle and wore faded Dashikis. He was a regular at pan-African meetings throughout the city. He began his day by reviewing countless magazine and newspaper articles. "You cannot be in the world and not know what the world is up to!" he would say to his friends. He had a knack for reading between the lines in analyzing world events and would frequently uncover covert activities that the media left out.

Ras hired Ra Heru Khuti as an apprentice at his printery, located on Lenox Ave and 138th Street, across from Liberation Book Store. Ra Heru Khuti loved being around Anpu and the rest of the crew. After work, in the evening, they would all gather around a bottle of Thunderbird which he kept hidden below his desk, under stacks of old newspapers. As the machines timed out, except the old printer in the back which Anpu keep running day and night, the plastic cups would appear out of the men's pockets; they would pop open the bottle and the debates would flow. Ras owned one of the first A.B. Dick two-color press with a Didde Apollo web press but dreamt of owning a five color perfector, either the Ryobi or the Shinohara. These presses would increase his business beyond his dreams. On a warm summer evening, when the sunset still peeped through the cracks in the walls of the old building and the dust filled the room in a dance of particles, Anpu was the loudest on the issue of reparations.

"Black people are not the only people who are demanding reparations." Anpu argued, throwing his hands wildly in the air like a conductor before his orchestra. Anpu's audience hung attentively on his every word.

"West Germany paid Jewish people for crimes committed during World War II. The US Government paid Japanese Americans for crimes against them in World War II. The Trans Atlantic slave trade made Europe rich; yet African people never received a cent for the atrocities committed against them. In fact, we were jailed just for filing a petition for reparations."

Ra Heru Khuti was still on the floor, unconscious, after passing out from drinking the Thunderbird which Anpu had also mixed with something else without informing him. Anpu continued his argument for reparations. When Ra Heru Khuti awoke, his head was against Pharaoh's boot that smelled like burnt rubber. He sat up with his back against the wall and vowed never again to drink another drop of alcohol. The tight band of pain that encircled his forehead now shifted to the back of his head. Still dazed, he stumbled to his feet by bracing against the wall, which gave in against the pressure of his uncontrolled body. Apparently the old crusted cement had broken off from the edges of the concrete blocks. The blocks crashed to the floor, accompanied with a downpour of dust and debris. Ra Heru Khuti was covered in dust as he coughed and brushed off his clothes. The dust eventually cleared away revealing a dusty black scroll with the words "*Papyrus Am Tuat*" and some hieroglyphic art inscribed in gold on its cover. "What the..?" Ra Heru Khuti started to say but caught himself.

"What a strange place for a scroll!" he thought as he reached behind the wall for it. He retrieved the scroll from the debris and dusted it off as a strange feeling came over him. Ra Heru Khuti experienced what can be described as an electrical shock that radiated throughout his body. His knees buckled under him and he saw a flash from his past life on *Mount Behutet* fighting with Sethe to protect the *Papyrus Am Tuat* from Sethe and his family. Tears dropped from his eyes. He knew not why he was crying but instantly the tears flowed. Carefully, he wiped the cover clean with his tears until the bold gold letters gradually became clearer. Some of the letters were missing but enough remained to reveal the title of the *Papyrus Am Tuat.* He could tell from the glyphics that the text was old, perhaps, even ancient. Glancing around suspiciously, he concealed the *Papyrus Am Tuat* under his clothing, close to his chest and made his way to the men's room.

He was still thumbing through the Papyrus when there was a slight tap on the door. He ignored it the first time but the tap was repeated again and again. "Will be right out!" he yelled as he hid the *Papyrus Am Tuat* in his clothing under his shirt a second time. He flushed the toilet, turned on and off the faucet, and opened the door pretending he was still wiping his hands. There was no one at the door. He walked past the drunken voices still belaboring the point and headed toward the door, trying to make his exit to the street undetected.

As he exited he could feel Anpu's eyes on him and avoided looking in his direction. Anpu had seen him pull the *Papyrus Am Tuat* from the wall and watched Ra Heru Khuti as he hid it in his chest under his garment on his way to the men's room.

"There are some books that should not be read!" Anpu simply remarked, "the kind of books that just having them can turn your world upside down. Mysterious things, accidents, unexplained things happen."

Ra Heru Khuti stared at Anpu. It was as if another person was speaking through him. His voice was unusually old and wise. Was it possible that Anpu had received a flash from his past life like Ra Heru Khuti had done when he touched the papyrus scroll. "If it wasn't meant to be read, then why write it?" Ra Heru Khuti gestured at the older man.

"Gimme got ya!" Anpu explained. "They will find you, and then what? Before you touched it you had a chance, but now they will find you. There is a reason why the press that printed that papyrus is no longer in business." The rest of them looked on as if the conversation was unreal. Anpu continued, "There are people in this world who have knowledge of human nature and seek to exploit it. Do you understand what I am saying? Predictions of things to come!!!" Ra Heru Khuti could not tell if these were the ramblings of a drunken old man or whether Anpu was in fact speaking profoundly!

"Do you understand? The book explains in detail how to harness and focus the most powerful earthly energies. If you don't have the correct understanding of how this ancient wisdom can affect your life, I suggest you put that scroll back where you found it!" Anpu insisted in a stern voice. It was no longer the old wise voice. It became a stern threatening voice.

"What do you know of these things drunk man?" Ra Heru Khuti asked him.

"A drunken man says what a sober person thinks! Predictions of things to come," he replied stroking his black and gray beard.

Ra Heru Khuti pulled the papyrus out from under his shirt and again wiped the cover with his forearm. Slowly, he read aloud the title. "What is the *Papyrus Am Tuat*?" he asked Anpu. Just the mention of the title made Anpu fall reverently to his knees with his hands clutching his heart. A silver white beam of light shone into the room, stopped directly over the papyrus and illuminated the book. The empty bottle of Thunderbird shattered as it hit the floor.

"What are you willing to give up? That's what they are asking!" Anpu begged of him shading his eyes from the light that shone as bright as two thousands suns.

Ra Heru Khuti, on the other hand, felt drawn to the *Papyrus Am Tuat* as if it had become his personal guide, his destiny or his purpose in life. Ra Heru Khuti was experiencing a strange connection to the scroll. He felt like he had participated in writing the *Papyrus Am Tuat* and it belonged to him. He could not explain it but he heard himself saying to Anpu as he headed toward the door, "I found my life!"

"No!" Sethe insisted emerging from the light and grabbing hold of his hand without restraining him. But Ra Heru Khuti felt Sethe's cold, lifeless hands and began to utter a chant that came to his lips *"Phats!"* With his purifying chant he was able to slide out of Sethe's grip.

Chapter 8: Sethian Empire

"How did you mess that up?" a venomous, gruff voice snarled at him. He looked up to see the furious glare of his grandfather, Mortimer Sethe leering down at him. Quickly, Sethe the younger tried to regain his grip, but he just as quickly stumbled and fell. "Get yourself together and catch up. We will soon have this young charlatan within our grasp, and I want you to see how we treat a thief."

His grandfather Mortimer Sethe was about to move on until he spied something on his descendant's chest. He faced him fully and then pointed to the dirty footprint on the front of Sethe the younger's shirt. He dropped a piece of paper on his chest with a word scribed in the ancient Canaanite that is often attributed to the Hebrews. "I trust that you have been educated in this ancient tongue?"

Sethe looked at the symbols and replied, "I believe this is the seal of Enoch!"

Sethe's father, Sethe the elder, guffawed "What seal of Enoch? It is a list of our confederacy through the ages" with that he waved his hand at him and a burning sensation engulfed Sethe's left forearm. Sethe's father smiled. "This is the first of the three that have been with you since you were born." Sethe's father turned over his arm and looked at the three red, glowing-hot Canaanite letters and numbers that appeared on the young man's forearm. A dark cloud came over his features. "We really must have that *Papyrus Am Tuat*." Sethe's father sighed in resignation as he flipped his grandson's arm back towards him.

"Recite this when you find him." Sethe's father then leaned in close so that his eyes looked deep down into Sethe's ear. "Now listen to this and listen carefully." He looked through him with disdain as he forcefully pronounced each word and wagged his finger in his face. "If you ever let another Shemsu Heru walk over you again, our family, and our fraternity will disgrace and disown you!" and with that he turned on his heel and disappeared in the direction of the pride.

"That was probably the last of them." Ra Heru Khuti thought to himself. With that he rose from his hiding place and proceeded to walk in the opposite direction. Just as he turned the corner to his house, Sethe turned the corner and caught a glimpse of his pant leg. He came to the corner, peered around the corner and suddenly a barrage of fists accosted him. Sethe wilted onto his backside, cowering behind his upraised left arm, marked with the name on the paper his grandfather had given him.

As Ra Heru Khuti raised his hand above his head, Sethe chanted the word under his breath, "Apep!" Suddenly in front of him Stinking Face, a.k.a. Apep, appeared - a tall, muscular, blond haired man with smoky red eyes. Apep wore his hair in long golden locks, but in an unusual style. His locks were tied into two big braids and the two braids were tied into one. They looked like ram horns. He carried a wooden club in his hand with what looked like a ram's head attached to the end. It was as if he was a standard bearer.

Apep took a step forward, shrugged Ra Heru Khuti's arms off his massive shoulders and then calmly looked back with a burning flame in his eyes. Ra Heru Khuti, out powered and out numbered, sped up the block. "Quickly follow him and inform my grandfather about where he lives!" Sethe frantically blurted out.

With that Apep smiled, "For the record, you owe me one," as he turned on his heels and was gone.

Sethe approached Ra Heru Khuti's house with a wild fury in his eyes. Apep stood at the doorway with his huge arms spread wide and glared down at his master. He chuckled to himself "This hovel is where the charlatan resides."

Sethe's father grabbed his son's face and studied the shiner that engulfed his left eye and the lump in the center of his forehead. He flipped it away brusquely and responded with a surly "Good job. Now go in there and find out the whereabouts of the *Papyrus Am Tuat* that thief took. The rest of you search the house from top to bottom."

A surge of fear rose up from the base of Sethe's spine and engulfed his head in a bough of dark water from which smaller streams reached towards the house like tentacles.

Apep smiled mischievously, "Would you like me to handle this matter?"

Sethe breathed a sigh of relief, "Would you, really?"

"Why of course, that is why I am here! Follow me." Apep responded with enthusiasm. Apep immediately burst through the door and began to fly down the hall into the house and then flipped over without stopping so he faced Sethe briefly. "It is going to cost you though."

Ra Heru Khuti looked back at the door with trepidation as he grabbed a bat and moved towards the sound.

"Where do you think you are going young man?" His mother Amseth demanded.

Ra Heru Khuti looked at his mother and his grandmother who were both large and formidable women. "I can't let him get to you two."

"I appreciate the sentiment, but that is not your job yet. No, son, that responsibility falls on me." A wry smile crept across his grandmother's face. She continued, "Look, I know a little more about these matters than you. I was expecting him. After all, I use the *Metu Neter* Oracle, remember?"

"What does that have to do with your risking your life for me?" Ra Heru Khuti pleaded in desperation. "You don't understand Mut. What I took really belongs to us but these guys will do anything to get it back!"

"Hold on. You are the only male but you are not the man of the house! But that does not take away from your eventual importance. You have a destiny young man and you must live to fulfill it! Take your time and lay the foundation in your spirit first. You will begin to understand your purpose in life as you realize the different aspects of your being. Then you will be prepared to fight Sethe and his followers with clarity and power."

"Yea, I know. Prophecies to fulfill! I am not leaving you!" With that she threw him out and locked the door. Immediately he flew towards the door and tried to get back in.

Behind the closed door, there was another crash, and he heard his mother scream and then someone collapsed onto the floor. His grandmother snatched him up by his shirt collar and dragged him out of the room, slamming the door shut. In the corridor, he could hear Amseth's laughter. Then the laughter stopped. He heard loud banging, and then he heard her scream. Ra Heru Khuti struggled to get free but his grandmother had a firm grip on him. "No!" he cried out and wrestled to get away, calling,

"Amseth! Amseth!" He pleaded with her pointing to the door where the screaming had subsided. "Amseth!" he cried, as his grandmother lifted him and held him tightly to her bosom. She ran down the stairs and into the night jumping over objects without a second thought. There was a man standing in front of the house under the streetlight, looking into the room. He, too, had heard Amseth's screams.

"Help! Help her please!" Ra Heru Khuti cried struggling in his grandmother's arms to get free.

He cried as the machete lashed out at her again and again and again.

"Please! Help!" he screamed as Amseth's blood splashed against the glass windows. His screams faded and everything seemed to have gone askew. They were somewhere out in the dark night, running. Lights and voices flashed by. Dogs were barking. People seemed to be running in every direction. He felt he was going to suffocate as his grandmother juggled him between her arms, squeezing him to her bosom, her heart beating dangerously. They fled through the night as Apep clubbed Amseth incessantly. Sethe the elder stood to the side whispering into the ears of Sethe the younger as he sat with his legs crossed swaying to and fro while taunting Amseth for information, "Tell me where the scroll is and this will stop" But Amseth continued to defy him and cried out in terrible pain.

"Herukhti-Ang! Herukhti-Ang!" In her suffering, she called upon her son to ease her pain.

Apep snorted loudly as he continued to pummel her at a workman's pace. Some of Sethe's followers were tearing apart the house looking for the papyrus.

"It hurts me to see your pain Amseth. Tell us where Ra Heru Khuti is hiding and Apep will end this quickly," Sethe reiterated deliberately. The movement of his lips and the words mirrored what flowed out of those of his grandfather. Suddenly there was a sickening crunch as Apep's fist grabbed her hair and the other hand held the bloody club high above her head. Hesitating briefly, he looked up at Sethe for the final command.

"Her life is in your hands." Sethe the elder whispered and nodded his head to Apep.

Chapter 9: Gangsta Rhymes

Stepping drums lined Fulton Street. Wind stalkers' rhymes and neon lights blended melodies with Sambas and shekeres to create night moods. "Blues is when yo' woman left you for your best buddy, so you choose to go on living with this hurt. This is called blues." Sammy Hawkins had his audience spell bound to his guitar howling of Bessie Smith's "Fat Women Need Love Too." Outside the bar room, street musicians clashed with night songs and the music of their interlock rocked the broken images. Unsolicited gangster rhymes sigh against the rugged metropolis. Natty Dread Youngbloods, their failing ambitions knotted against barbed wire fences, glare at gang Lords riding about in uniforms, "Dread-a-War" erupting off their lips.

Xanadu was a paralysis of flickering strobe lights and cool rhythmic music of Blue Magic. The night club was crowded. On the dance floor wire-waisted men and women pulverized by the soulful Philadelphia sounds bathed in the astral climax. Their eyes gleamed with intoxication as their torsos imitated the whirl smoke dance of the cigarettes. Ra Heru Khuti felt out of place sitting among the half-naked women peddling sex and drunken men who all seemed to be acting out of their minds. But Apep insisted they meet at the bar called the Tuat Den.

Ra Heru Khuti ordered a glass of ginger ale and pretended to be a part of the scene until he was told to get up from the bar unless he ordered a real drink. He ordered a rum and coke and it sat in front of him. Soon after, Apep and Sethe arrived. Ra Heru Khuti jumped up and stormed toward them blinded by his desire for revenge for what they had done to Amseth. Apep, always ready for combat, responded. He lashed out at Ra Heru Khuti with a machete. Ra Heru Khuti blocked with one arm and struck Apep with his other hand, hitting him under the armpit and knocking him over the tables.

Apep recovered, scrambled to his feet and in one quick movement, swept the glass off the counter and poured the rum and coke down his throat. "Thanks," he said belching in Ra Heru Khuti's face. "We love, we care, but business is business." Sethe, tall, thin, blonde with freckles on his cheeks hid his eyes behind his dark sunshades. Sethe advanced toward Ra Heru Khuti and stared at him in his eyes "You have something that belongs to me!" Apep moved threatenly closer to Ra Heru Khuti.

"What might that be?" Ra Heru Khuti teased.

Sethe, anticipating his response, replied, "I am willing to pay you handsomely for that document. It's been in my family for at least two generations. When the temple was burned we thought we had lost it. Now you found it. Return it to us! Name your price?" Sethe proposed facing Ra Heru Khuti and staring into his eyes.

"You will never get the *Papyrus Am Tuat* from me alive," Ra Heru Khuti continued. "You say this document has been in your family for at least two generations. I would say it's been in someone else's family for at least three thousand years prior since it dates back to about 5000 BC. How does that make it yours?" Ra Heru Khuti asked him.

"You wear my patience," Sethe said to Ra Heru Khuti as he stood up from the bar. "I have no time for this." He placed a fifty dollar bill on the counter, told the bartender to keep the change and snarled at Apep on his way out the door.

"Get me my *Papyrus Am Tuat*. I don't care what it takes. Get it and bring it to the house. I am depending on you!" His words were enough to ignite Apep who stormed toward Ra Heru Khuti.

"You heard the man!" Ra Heru Khuti felt a dull heavy blow against his cheek and collapsed on the floor. His legs could not sustain the weight of his body. He felt a pair of strong arms around his waist and knew Apep was maneuvering his body to place him in a bear hug. He struggled to avoid the grip tightening against his waist but felt his energy waning. There were more voices. Shots were fired. There was a massive scramble and he knew he was fainting.

That's when Ifa Dare showed up. With his martial arts and military background he confronted Apep. Both men stared into each others eyes, both possessing killing skills far beyond those of the average person. Ifa Dare with cat-like swiftness swung and kicked at Apep until the tall and muscular man fell. But in a moment Apep was back on his feet shaking it off. He blew smoke out of his mouth and disappeared into it.

Ifa Dare held his posture, closed his eyes and in words, unknown to Ra Heru Khuti, called upon his ancestors to intervene. He tapped his foot three times and Apep reappeared, slashing the air with his blade. Ifa Dare again moved with blinding speed to counteract his attack and blew some liquid out of his mouth into Apep's face. Staggering backward, Apep started spinning around in a wild craze. In a flash, Ifa Dare grabbed Ra Heru Khuti and dragged him toward the door. Outside, they ran furiously, stopping only once to catch their breath.

"Got to move on. They will be all over this place in a minute," Ifa Dare urged as he sprinted ahead.

A patrol car slowly drove by. Ra Heru Khuti could see his silhouette against the building, as Apep's black van circled the block. Suddenly, everything seemed to happen all at once. A parked Buick blinked its lights. A man appeared at one end of the corner. He was yelling and waving at someone as he ran toward a red Mustang parked opposite the Buick. Both the patrol car and the Buick then chased the red Mustang. Ifa Dare stepped out of the doorway and pushed Ra Heru Khuti in the opposite direction. They walked at a moderate pace for two blocks then Ifa Dare hailed a cab. They took the cab across town to the Flatbush Avenue neighborhood where Ifa Dare was renting an apartment in the Ebbet's Field Apartment Complex in Brooklyn.

Inside the apartment, Ifa Dare retrieved a small brown bottle from the medicine cabinet and gave it to Ra Heru Khuti, "Here! Take some!" The bottle said Rescue Remedy. There wasn't much information on the yellow colored label except the usual warning.

"Squeeze a few drops under your tongue and rub some of this on that bump at the side of your head!" Ifa Dare instructed him, also giving him a tube of Arnica ointment.

"How you know so much about medicine?" Ra Heru Khuti asked him.

"How come you ask so many questions?" Ifa Dare asked in return.

"The Obi says we should go see Shekhem Kesnu Neter. He will tell us what to do with the *Papyrus Am Tuat* and how to handle Sethe and his men." The manner in which Ifa Dare said this made Ra Heru Khuti respect his wish. Ra Heru Khuti sat back and watched Ifa Dare divine with the bones. Ifa Dare could recite countless Odu. He trusted his divination skills. Ra Heru Khuti also knew Shekhem Kesnu Neter when he visited his Het Neter in Harlem, New York City. He was very much impressed with his divination skills. He laid his head on the couch, feeling very relaxed, knowing the next day he would receive counsel from the great Shekhem Kesnu Neter. Shekhem Kesnu Neter headed the Harlem Hesp that had a very large following. The Shekhem was known for his Qi Gong skills. He had healed several people from various illnesses by the mere touch of his palm. Often, the Het Neter was so crowded they had to turn away visitors from their monthly lunar meditations that the Shekhem Kesnu Neter presided over and displayed possessions in great measure. He went so deep into trance that whomever he touched was healed of their affliction. Ra Heru Khuti couldn't wait to meet the Shekhem in person. "We going to Harlem?" Ra Heru Khuti asked, but Ifa Dare was already asleep.

Chapter 10: America's Most Wanted

As they exited from the FDR Drive on to 125th Street, Ra Heru
Khuti had a bad feeling about going to Harlem. Harlem always
seemed to hit him like the worst hangover. It never seemed real.
Ifa Dare was from Harlem. He knew everyone in Harlem. They
pulled up to Fifth Avenue to grab a bite to eat at the Ital Juice
Bar. As they parked, a green Mercedes, with gold plated rims
and tinted glass, double parked next to them.

"Who dat?" asked Ifa Dare. The look of concern on his face
diminished as the tinted glass slowly rolled down revealing a set
of gold teeth and dark glasses.

The face was hidden under a baseball cap. Junebug smiled,
nodding his head toward Ifa Dare, "What up? You must be going
on dat boat ride."

Ifa Dare got out the car and walked over to the Mercedes, "It's
all good. Going to see the righteous man. How's business?" On
the passenger side of the car sat Mo Deep, Junebug's partner. Mo
Deep was the muscle for Junebug. He was tall, dark and sexy
chocolate. The women called him African dark. But he never
smiled. He sported a clean shaven head and a thick moustache.

He sat back with a bag full of hundred dollar bills in his lap. Next to his leg lay an Uzi semiautomatic. Ifa Dare looked at the hundreds as they slipped through his fingers.

"What yo looking at?" Mo Deep snapped at him peeking over his sunglasses. Ifa Dare knew Mo Deep from back when they used to run together in the Convent. Mo Deep was crazy. He wasn't going to mess with him.

On the other side of 125th Street, Sebek ran out of the Burger King joint with the manager chasing him. Sebek had ordered two burgers and ran out of the store when the salesgirl was getting the drinks, but the manager and owner, Jagdeo from India, spotted him and gave chase. Sebek ran around cars, swung through the Bernie's Used Furniture Store, climbed the fence and lay in the grass knowing Jagdeo wasn't going to climb the fence. Jagdeo gave chase until he got to the fence, cursed Sebek and turned back. Five minutes later Sebek was back on 125th Street. He had eaten the burgers and now he wanted something to wash them down. He eyed the green Mercedes as a possible source of cash.

As Sebek approached the Mercedes, Junebug spotted him and quickly told Mo Deep, "Don't let him come over here!"

Mo Deep got out of the car and when Sebek saw him, he stopped in his tracks. "Git!" Mo Deep shouted at him.

Sebek paused for moment reconsidering his position and cried out to Mo Deep "Ah, C'mon Mo, we go way back… help a brotha out!" Mo Deep pulled his other hand out of the car revealing the Uzi.

Sebek took off down the block. Meanwhile no one saw the black Corvette pulling up to the Mercedes. By the time Mo Deep turned around from being distracted by Sebek, the windows were down in the Corvette and a nine millimeter was pointing out the window.

"Mo!" Junebug shouted diving for cover. The nine millimeter had already squirted its deadly bullets into Mo Deep who staggered holding his stomach. The Corvette sped away, its tires squeaking.

Everyone was in shock. Ifa Dare looked down at Junebug on the ground. He wasn't moving. "Junior!" he screamed, shaking him. As he rolled him over, Junebugs' chest was covered in blood. He was shot right through the heart. On the floor of the Mercedes was the bag full of money. "Hell No!" Ifa Dare said. No way he was gonna let them dirty cops get hold of this. He reached over, grabbed the bag and threw it into the back seat of his car. He also knew Junebug, kept his stash under the back seat. He opened the back door and under the seat, Bingo! He grabbed the two bags and ran to his car. The sirens were getting closer. "Drive!" he shouted to Ra Heru Khuti who panicked and slammed the car in reverse. He adjusted the gear and sped off. "Easy! Easy!" Ifa Dare coached him, "Drive normal. You definitely don't want to draw attention!" Ra Heru Khuti slowed the car, eased onto Lexington Avenue and headed down to 116th Street.

"What luck!" Ifa Dare thought. He knew Junebug's boys would be up and rollin' in a minute. But who would want Junebug dead? That was a bold move. As they turned on 116th Street, cars sped up. Ifa Dare knew it was too late. He quickly started pulling out rolls of hundreds out of two of the bags, cut a split in the seat and stuffed the money inside. He took off his shirt and covered the seat. As he sat back down he noticed the two cars at the intersection. "Oh Darn!" he uttered. The light changed but the cars remained. He drove into the middle of the two cars. "Wher' G Shine at?" he called to the driver.

"What you want?" the voiced called back. Four more cars pulled up surrounding them. From the far side of the street, a tall, skinny, light skinned and clean shaven man approached the car. Ifa Dare would not have noticed him except for the fact he held a nine millimeter beside his leg. He looked into the car, saw the bags and waved in the direction of the last four cars that pulled up. He opened the back door and slid into the back seat. "Drive! Follow that car!" he instructed, pointing the gun toward the brown Lexus. They followed the cars along Lenox Avenue. They drove up to the 145th Street Bridge, crossed into the Bronx and ended up on Woody Crest Avenue. G Shine walked over to the car.

G Shine was one of America's most wanted. Back in the day he ran a gang out of the West Bronx that terrorized even the local cops. He had killed a few people, including two cops, over some drug deals and quickly became one of America's most wanted. The thing is, the cops knew where he lived but everyone was scared to arrest him. G Shine's control was wide and all encompassing. Local cops, correction officers, doctors and judges were on his bankroll. He had a slight limp in his right leg. "What up dog!" he greeted Ifa Dare, slapping fives. "Who dis fool? And what happened?" he asked, looking at Ra Heru Khuti.

"Dis is a good friend. We were on our way to see the Righteous Man when Junebug pulled up. We were catching up on some things when dis black Corvette suddenly pulled up and sprayed the place. Mo and Junior bought it. I didn't want dem dirty cops to get hold of his stash, so I grabbed it and took off. I know Junior Mom's could use some of it." Ifa Dare answered.

G Shine took off his sunglasses and looked him in the eye, "Looka her'. Dis ain't about the money. Did you get a look at the driver?" he asked him.

Ifa Dare thought deeply for a moment. He closed his eyes and recalled the scene in his mind's eyes. "No! I didn't see the face I only saw the nine millimeter.

"Yo grab dat!" G Shine told one of the men pointing to the bags of money and walking toward the house.

"What about dem? Want us to take care of 'em?" The light skinned young man who sat in the back seat inquired, pointing his gun in their direction.

"Na let 'em go." G Shine motioned to Ifa Dare. "You did Ok. Go see the Righteous Man! And give him my regards," he told Ifa Dare reaching into his pocket and pulling out two thick rolls of hundreds. "Dis for your troubles." He handed the rolls to Ifa Dare who refused to take them. G Shine insisted, so he relented.

As Ifa Dare and Ra Heru Khuti took off, G Shine shouted at them "See ya on the boat ride!"

What boat ride? Ra Heru Khuti thought, glancing at the two black Mercedes Benz cars that pulled up in front of G Shine's house. He immediately recognized Sethe and Apep who was still wearing dark sun glasses. "Look! Look!" he shouted to Ifa Dare pointing to Sethe. They pulled on Sherwood Street, crossed Jerome Avenue and turned on to Grand Concourse.

Chapter 11: Going to Meet

Shekhem Kesnu Neter turned out to be everything Ra Heru Khuti expected him to be. They were ushered in through a maze of doors and stairways until they ended up in a small room with three windows and two pieces of furniture. A desk and a chair stood in the middle of the room. Shekhem Kesnu Neter stood with his back toward them, gazing through the window that looked out on 125th Street.

"The United Nations said genocide is not simply the physical destruction of a people. It is defined also as cultural destruction. When you take away a person's name, language, religion, when you do your best to separate a man from his tradition, his culture, his ancient way of life, his community...that too is genocide!" Shekhem Kesnu Neter's eyes were still fixed on the half clad women and drug users hanging out at the corner of 125th Street. Across the street, Clap Hand Church was in session. The music of God's battalion was loud with its rhythmic melodies.

"What is a community but a dynamic spiritual factor," Shekhem Kesnu Neter continued gazing down at the streetwalkers below. "The majority of people are at the point in their lives where if they don't have social pressures and incentives within the community, they will not do Neter's work consistently."

Ra Heru Khuti knew he was referring to the street walkers and panhandlers who make 125th Street their business. They just met and the Shekhem seemed to be reading his thoughts. "How did he get to be who he is?" Ra Heru Khuti wondered. He was said to be a sage, a wise and holy man.

"Shekhem Kesnu Neter is to Africa America what Krishna is to the East, Buddha to Asia, Christ to the West and Mohammed to the Middle East." Ifa Dare said with pride.

Ra Heru Khuti considered himself to be fortunate. How many people in the world have an opportunity to get counsel from a sage? To gain insight into their lives? To receive wise counsel as to who to marry, what education to get, what job to do? To avoid the blunders of wrong decision making in life?

Ra Heru Khuti had heard that after mastering concert piano, Shekhem Kesnu Neter had a vision of leading his people back to the ancient wisdom of their ancestors. He was studying for a career as a concert pianist when he received the word of God so he dropped the entertainment thing and began to do his sage thing. All of his friends and family thought he was crazy to give up such a promising career. Only his mother supported him. She was the only person who always held uncompromising confidence in him. When he told her of his decision, she smiled tears of joy and told him how proud she was that he had made such a wise decision.

Shekhem Kesnu Neter continued, "When you attain to who you are, you have power over your life, over things on Earth. Our reaction to the world, one of illusion, is based on conditioned responses. You come to learn and see that the real work has to do with building and sustaining a community. Spiritual work is really nothing grand or fantastic. It has to do with simple things like being mindful of the thoughts and images you accept, providing a righteous environment whereby children can come into the world and realize their divine potential through everyday things like: healthy diet, quality schooling, righteous examples, harmonious homes for wives, husbands and children, and a peaceful social environment. In a nutshell, that's spiritual work. But most people consider spiritual work as something, above and beyond, something that involves action outside of our daily activities."

The Shekhem slowly turned to face them, "The real goal of spirituality is nothing more than perfecting oneself in a harmonious social environment. We cannot talk about all the higher spiritualities if we cannot live decently and honestly and sincerely and lovingly in peace and harmony with each other.

That's the proof in the pudding. All these other things are means to that end. I am not saying they are not important. That's why we are given our physical vehicles, so that God can come into the world and experience it through us. Yes, you must go through them, you must know about them, you must work with them, you must be able to manipulate all those higher forces into a harmonious fellowship as the true expression of oneness."

"Oneness! Ha! So many organizations and nations dream of Oneness! But not one of them have attained it except for a few individuals here and there!" Ra Heru Khuti thought. But again, the Shekhem read his mind.

"How do we come to live in harmony with each other, in harmony with ourselves, in harmony with the divine law? That's another discussion." He walked over to Ifa Dare who slightly bowed to him and pointing his fingers in the direction of the Shekhem's heart, tapped the back of his right hand into his left palm three times make a slapping sound *"Anetch Hrak!"*

Ra Heru Khuti had seen other people greet the Shekhem this way before and never asked why they greeted him in this special manner.

The Shekhem returned the greeting saying *"Hrak Hetepu!"*

Ra Heru Khuti did not know what the greeting meant but he felt such an overwhelming respect and humility in his presence, he quickly imitated Ifa Dare's gestures, clumsily tapping the back of his right hand unto his left palm. The Shekhem smiled, extending his hand toward Ra Heru Khuti and making him more comfortable. Ra Heru Khuti took his hand and immediately felt a calmness descending upon him. It was strange. How would merely touching someone generate such calm and peace and love? He heard of such things before but to experience it from a Black man in America. Wow!

Ifa Dare gestured toward Ra Heru Khuti. "Sethe found out the *Papyrus Am Tuat* was in his possession and came after him. We saw him meeting with G-Shine. We came to seek counsel on what to do with the Papyrus?"

"You want me to consult the great oracle of the *Metu Neter* for this? Are you sure that's what you came for?" The Shekhem replied. The *Metu Neter* Oracle came down to African Americans in 1982. It was an historic event. The *Metu Neter* Oracle or Word of God was given to Africans in America, in the same way the great I Ching was prominent among the Chinese, the Ifa dominated Yoruba life, the Tarot was magic to the European and the Kabala to the Jews.

Ifa Dare had heard the rumor that when the European and Arab grave robbers pillaged Egypt during the early nineteenth century, whenever they dug up the tombs of the Pharaohs, they found this very *Papyrus Am Tuat*. The Shekhem spoke with reverence of such historic antecedents.

"In Kamit, when you died they would speak about those spiritual things that you accomplished upon the Earth. It was an enthroned practice to bury with you those chapters of spiritual development that you mastered on this Earth. Those chapters of the *Papyrus Am Tuat* were buried with you. There were inscriptions of words and magical rituals to keep you from getting lost during your living on the Earth, and words of wisdom to keep your heart from being stolen from you by giving in to the five emotions. Words of wisdom assist you through all the mysterious gates in your path on your journey to the light from whence you came. Every person who has taken the time to study spiritual culture has learned that life on Earth prepares you for your life after death. So, there is nothing that you can do in the after life unless you accomplished it while alive. As above so below." The Shekhem's words were beginning to vibrate in him. Ra Heru Khuti glanced over at Ifa Dare.

"This *Papyrus Am Tuat* was part of the 11 Laws: Maa Kheru, which dealt with the process of becoming whole again. If you pass this process successfully you will then go forth by day. Meaning you will have the light of enlightment ahead of you. The *Papyrus Am Tuat* is talking about you. You are still dead if you are not awakened to the light. The dead is impotent. The divine within your spirit is not alive yet. That is why you are impotent, that's why little emotions assault and control you here and there. That is why you don't benefit from your omniscience. Your knowledge is partial because the wisdom faculty within you is dormant, dead or asleep."

Ifa Dare interrupted the Shekhem. "So the *Papyrus Am Tuat* is really about your spiritual power, isn't it? What does it mean when it says 'not having your heart stolen from you?" He asked the Shekhem. Ifa Dare, obviously had read the *Papyrus Am Tuat*. "Listen to people talk. Every day we have people crying, 'I fell in love,' 'you stole my heart,' 'I love you with all my heart,' 'I hate you,' 'I can't…' These are metaphors for saying you were swept away by emotion, by your desire, by your passion. You say 'I lost my heart or my head.' So people say you feel with your heart and think with the head, so when you are swept away by feelings you have lost your heart. This comes from the ancient knowledge that there is something within you called the heart, not the physical heart but a psychic center located within the breast that has connections with the heart. That is why you are emotional when your heart beats quickly because the heart is energetically connected to that psychic center. When this psychic center begins to function on a higher level it makes the heart beat very quickly. The *Papyrus Am Tuat* warns about the dangers of having your heart stolen from you by the demons. The demon or evil is also a metaphor for one of those emotional desires, and passions that make you act irrationally and emotionally instead of acting with reason. Black people, the ancient Egyptians were very poetic. Since antiquity Black people have mastered the metaphoric use of words." His words were measured.

Ra Heru Khuti was burning up. He could no longer restrain his curiosity. "You mean the ancient Egyptians who produced these teachings were Black?" he asked the Shekhem with excitement.

"Of course! They are your ancestors. That's what the whole Sethe thing is about. It's about not letting you know your history…keeping you ignorant!" Shekhem Kesnu Neter said, like it was no big thing. But it shook Ra Heru Khuti's world. He grew up, like most people, associating Black history with the slave trade or the Civil Rights Movement, not realizing the history of African Americans began thousands of years ago. Worse than that, many Black people don't even know who they are. He listened intensely, glued to every word that came out of the Shekhem's mouth.

"When you think of Black people, many people think of Africa. That's a mistake. When you push your history far back enough, you find that what today is Southern China, India, Southern Europe, Palestine, Northern Syria, were all occupied by

Black people, long before the Chinese and the Caucasian people came," Shekhem Kesnu Neter said.

It was clear to Ra Heru Khuti why hundreds of people lined up every week to hear Shekhem Kesnu Neter speak. Every word was awakening something in him. He didn't want it to end.

"What should I do with the *Papyrus Am Tuat*?" Ra Heru Khuti asked when he found words again.

The Shekhem shuffled the *Metu Neter* Oracle cards, reached for one and turned it over. He repeated the action flicking over another card. He then closed his eyes, leaned back and sank his breath. "You need to cross the great waters. All things arise from the same energy and matter, to ultimately serve the same purpose. They have a common divine mother and father. Fear not, for he who harms another, harms himself."

The Shekhem did another reading and said "He who knows the way to the sage knows the way to the highest aspect of his being. Get on that boat and go to the city of Men Nefer and find the blind sage called Kheper Aunghkti. He is expecting you." He told Ra Heru Khuti rising from the table.

"What boat and what about the *Papyrus Am Tuat*?" Ra Heru Khuti asked. He had heard of the twin cities of Anu and Men Nefer along the banks of the Delaware Water Gap.

"The *Papyrus Am Tuat*, accompanying you in your sojourn here in the Tuat, was the original copy taken from the sarcophagus of the Shekhem Ur Shekhem Unas of the Fifth Dynasty. Sethe had John Henry, the reputable archaeologist, smuggled it out of Egypt. In 1822 Champollion decoded the Rosetta Stone and gave the European world the key to decipher the Egyptian hieroglyphs. Meaning that from the Fifth century AD until 1822, Europeans had a pseudo interpretation of the hieroglyphs. At the same time that they began to read the Egyptian monuments and understand for the first time what they were reading, they were impressed with the greatness they found. Subsequently, many Europeans were sent to Egypt and returned to Europe with great mathematical leaps in physics and in science. The Germans, followed by the French and Italians, did a lot of excavation.

The Rosetta Stone was a stone that had inscriptions in Greek, the name of Cleopatra, the name of Ptolemy, and a few other facts of the time, and the Egyptian version of it was translated side by side. So, they were able to make correspondences from Greek to Egyptian. And that was the key that enabled them to translate other Egyptian writings. This inscription made by Cleopatra and the Ptolemies was done in 196 BC.

The Free Masons, the Orthodox Jews and the Catholic Church studied and kept the first copy of the *Papyrus Am Tuat*. Then a second copy was translated, a more popular version where most of the rituals were left out. This second edition made it into the public domain. But the Vatican kept the first translation and allowed the Free Masons, the Elders of the Orthodox Jewish State and the Jesuit priests of the Catholic Church to study it and perform rituals.

In 1876, the Masons stole the copy of the *Papyrus Am Tuat* from the Vatican and hid it the Grand Lodge in Charleston, South Carolina under the vigilant eye of the then Grand Wizard, Mortimer Sethe, the grandfather of Sethe. Mortimer Sethe later moved to New York City and bought a place in downtown Manhattan which later became known as Harlem where he maintained his extensive private collection of stolen artifacts from Egypt. He hosted social gatherings in the basement of his home and invited representatives from the Grand Knights Templar, the Rosicrucians, the Martinists, the Knights of Columbus, the Elks, the Rotary and many others. They often served up freshly exhumed mummies he maintained in his private collection as appetizers." Shekhem Kesnu Neter spoke rapidly as he walked them out to the street. "Maa Kheru! Maa Kheru!" he whispered to Ra Heru Khuti, as he waved goodbye.

Chapter 12: Hatti's Dream

Hatti had had her share of bad luck. It seems that her whole family had bad luck. Her mother was in Charleston, South Carolina, praying over the accidental deaths of her two grandchildren, struck and killed during a thunderstorm while visiting her. Her mother had just said "Amen" when a lighting bolt hit across the street, ran through a water pipe and exploded into her kitchen, knocking her down and killing her. Her father, pastor of the God's Battalion church, while praying for his Deacon's health, plunged to his death when the poorly supported floor of the church gave way.

Now, she sat looking upon her dead son in his casket with a semiautomatic gun in his hand and a blunt in his mouth. Friends and enemies came to verify that he was actually dead. Junebug had terrorized everyone he came in contact with.

Family members and friends approached the coffin, held their hats in their hands, gazed into the coffin for a moment, stiffened, put their hats back on and nodded in her direction. Occasionally, someone would slip a thick padded roll of dollar bills into her hand.

A young woman stood by his body and was so overwhelmed with grief that she had to be taken outside. She leaned against the hearse parked outside sobbing and dabbing at her eyes. "He's the best person I've ever met," she cried. "To know him was to love him." She recalled how Junebug would sing to her and tell jokes or call her "Jig."

Outside the sanctuary, in the foyer was a collage of photos of Junebug. One was from his high school graduation: huge gazelle glasses, a hand clasping his basketball, a broad smile. There was a professional portrait of his family. Yet another picture showed him with his little brothers sitting on his knees, a goofy grin dominating his face.

They came by the hundreds from far and near, dressed in expensive sneakers, gold and diamond chains hanging down their chests. Some had matching earrings and teeth guards. They came from cities we have never heard of and towns we are too familiar with. They waited hours to say goodbye to Junebug, their fallen brother, gunned down in the prime of his life. Family and friends struggled to understand how the life of a dedicated, hardworking drug dealer came to such an abrupt, untimely and senseless end. Now his beautiful wife had no husband. Numerous chicken-heads no longer had a hustler to pay the rent, five boys no longer had a father, and siblings had one less brother. Parents had one less child; the local basketball league had one less investor. The entire population of the borough of Brooklyn had one less dealer on the streets to be afraid of.

As people lined the streets, his funeral procession left St. Francis Methodist Episcopal Church and headed for the Evergeen Cemetery. News helicopters hovered overhead. Motorcycle gangs lined the streets. First, it was the Crown Heights Bloods, then Bedford Stuyvesant, Bushwick, Red Hook, then Flatbush. The hearse followed. The family rode in the limousines paid for by Ojay. Then, an endless stream of Mercedes, BMW's and Jaguars-all custom made cars-came so fast it was hard to see with eyes full of tears.

"Apuat! I want to tell you my dream!" Hatti said to Apuat who was helping wash the dishes back at the house. Apuat was known to be at funerals and weddings. He always claimed to know the dead and the groom even though he didn't. To him it was a sure way of getting a good meal, free liquor and whatever else he could steal.

"As soon as I finish these dishes I am all ears," Apuat answered back from out of the kitchen.

"No, please come listen to my dream!" Hatti begged, seeming desperate.

"OK!" Apuat agreed, after he had poured himself another glass of palm wine and came into the living room.

"Ok! You don't have to yell at Apuat! Apuat will listen to your dream!" he said sitting on the couch and spreading his legs open.

Hatti wrinkled her nose at the fermenting mixture of the wine and cigar smoke on his breath. She opened the window above her head and gazed out. A few beads of perspiration trickled from her armpits. She hugged her skirt between her legs and narrated her dream to Apuat.

I sit in front of my father's house watching my little sister, Mfuele, play in the mud. Today, I can look into the face of the sun. It is not as strong as yesterday. I can see it growing weak over the Bunani village to the Southeast. The clouds are threatening.

"Mfuele!" I say, "Do not play in the mud." Mfuele has a mind of her own though she is only three years old. She does whatever she wants. Maybe that is because she makes my father's heart smile. He tickles her with undying affection. My mother, Mnile, is bending over the fire grating corn. My mother is the most beautiful woman in Mkuosa.

"Olele!" she sings, "Olele!"

I notice something is wrong with the day, with the wind, with the way things are. I sit staring into the face of the sun trying to figure out what's wrong, but some great shadow keeps moving my mind.

"Mfuele!" I say again, "Do not play in the mud with your hands!" She picks up a stick and continues to play with the mud.

"Aaaaaah, that Mfuele!" my mother said. "Leave her alone" my mother tells me. "Why do you bother your sister?"

I look at my mother as she grates corn. She is so beautiful in the morning light, her hair hangs to the side of her face and she looks over her shoulder to smile at me. I love my mother so much. The women of Mkousa say my mother is Sile, the sunlight made of wind that caresses the morning dew. I still feel the great sky is disturbed and I rise to study it intensely when Mnifa comes running through the village.

"Mnile!" I called "Mnifa is running!" Soon the women are running after Mnifa, they are dressed in white cloth of Mkousa and screaming through the village. The other women come out of their homes and gather around Mnifa. The children, seeing their mothers occupied with Mnifa take advantage to play unsupervised. Mnifa is a big woman; she has strong breasts and wears her work with her. She is the most respected woman in Mkousa. Her head is always tied with white cloth that is knotted on the side. I can see her holding her loose skirt in her hands as she cries. Her words are sad. It is true her words are no longer hidden behind the great mountain of Mtongo. They come pouring freely from her lips. Now she gives her spirit freely of the great Ifa. She gestures to the sky.

"The great white horse comes!" She faces the sky with the courage of the ancestors of Mkousa gleaming in her face. Her courage is not defiant but steadfast. "The great white horse in the sky is storming to Mkousa." I look up to see Mnifa's vision. A mighty white horse galloping out of the sky to Mkousa, its big white blue eyes do not see what it's trampling. Its only concern is with galloping through the land. Look, it acts like it has never been freed before, so it gallops not because it has somewhere to go but because it is free to run. The white horse is heading straight for Mkousa. The clouds try to hold it back but it breaks them effortlessly. Mnifa warned the men before they left that it was useless. "They do not listen to the women." she tells the women gathered around her.

"Ajube! Ajube!" she called. Ajube traveled the land telling the history of the people of Mkousa, Funi, of Beri and Mtounga, of Itawaya and the great empire of the Oshosi people. He enters the villages when the sun is strong and the people gather. They welcome him with water to wash his feet along with beer to drink and food to eat. They offer him the special seat where he sits enthroned in white Biki robes. He sings and plays the Omnra which was handed down to him from his father and his father.

The children sit excitedly in front of the elder and he tells them the history of the people of Mkousa, Funi, of Beri and Mtounga, of Itawaya and the great empire of the Oshosi people. "Ajube! Ajube!" they called, "Tell us the history! Please comfort us."

"Today I tell you of the people of Mkousa." Ajube began, "This is very special story. I was born in Mkousa. This is the story of my people, of my family and the day the white horse came galloping toward Mkoussa."

"Oye! Oye! Abado! Ajube!" They responded. Mnifa's hand was the spear of Mkousa pointing to the pale blue eyes of the white horse.

"Oye Babajube, Mkousa! Jabala!" She counseled the white horse. The great Oracle of *Ifa* had foretold the coming of the white horse. Mnifa said the men should sit with Elegba and he would tell them how to defeat the great white horse. But the men would not listen. They say the spears of Mkousa are mighty in the sky. Had they not defeated the great Mdungi warriors whose shields were beyond the double horizons? They laughed. They would blind the white horse, before they cut off the legs, and then decapitate the rider. Then the mighty warriors would stab their spears into its belly and tear out its heart. This is the way of the Mkousa people. This is why the lions hide from the Mkousa people.

But Mnifa warned it would not be so! She said to go meet Elegba at the crossroad of Itngi, offer him sweet juba beans and

palm wine. Let the smoke from his pipe dance in the wind and he
will blow in your ears the weakness of the great white horse.

But the men would not listen to Mnifa. They met in the circle
under the Mkosi tree and they drank the lion's blood. Then they
smoked the leaves of Ndugo and their eyes were inflamed from
the fire breath of Mkosi. They hungrily ate fire as the flames
engulfed their bodies without burning them. Omnfuele, my
father, leader of the men of Mkousa, dug the teeth of the
conquered lions in his arms and jumped into the flames. When
the men caught his spear which flew through the night he swore
he would ride the back of the great white horse. They drummed
and Mkosi would not come.

"This is the way of Elegba!" Mnifa warns them. The men,
drunk with thunder call lightning into their being and storm off to
challenge the great white horse.

The women gathered still around Mnifa. They squeeze their
babies to their breasts. Across the fields I can see the horses
galloping toward the village. Their riders urge them on towards
the village. I stand unmoved. I am not afraid. But everything else
is afraid. The hens run wild and even the cocks begin to fly. The
cows refuse to feed and they run off to the woods. Yes, even the
animals know the slaughter of the great men of Mkousa in the
fields of Nitingi is imminent, and their conquerors are storming
toward the defenselss village. "I, Ajube, am truly the daughter of

the great Omnfuele, the Otumfo of Makousa. I shall not run. I shall call upon the spirit father, Mkosi, to fight the evil white horse."

"Mfuele! Do not be afraid!" I say to my sister as the Ogigi shoot my mother in the head. She rolls over on the ground with blood gushing out of her head.

"Kill them!" the Ogigi commands. One of the Ogigi steps down from his horse and walks toward Mfuele.

"Mfuele!" I say to her, "Do not be afraid. You will soon be with Mnile. Do not be afraid!"

The Ogigi shoots the flame into Mfuele. Her little lifeless body is flung a few feet by the force of the bullet. I can see the other Ogigi spearing the women as they call upon the great Mtongo to receive their spirits. The village of Mkousa goes up in flames.

"Ogigi!" I shout at the top of my voice, "I call upon the ancestors of the ancestors of the people of Mkousa, weavers of great cloth. I call upon the fire of Xgouxsi the mightiest of weapons to condemn you to the place of Oware – the place of white spirits where you shall live in blind torment wandering the caves of the distant mountains with nothing to eat!"

"Shut her up!" the Ogigi yells pointing at me.

The Ogigi that shot Mfuele comes toward me, aiming his weapon at my head. I continued to yell to the Ogigi, "I, Ajube of

Mkousa, daughter of Omnfuele, the great Otumfu do not know fear..."

Hatti's fingers were digging into Apuat's hands. Apuat, on the other hand, was biting into the cigar to ease the pain.

Chapter 13: Missing Black Boys

Ra Heru Khuti and Ifa Dare had just pulled up on Bedford
Avenue when they noticed Hatti running down the street toward
them with the Daily News in her hand. The morning newspaper
broke the news that the two boys were eaten by an alligator in
Prospect Park. The pathologist had discovered items belonging to
the boys in its belly. The boys were obviously both attacked and
dragged under the water by the alligator, where it ate them. She
ran barefooted. Her hair was wild all over her face and her
protruding hips swayed from side to side as she ran. She reached
the corner of Bedford and Crown, ran through the gas station and
was running back down Bedford when they turned on to Bedford
Avenue.

Hatti was hysterical. There were a number of people chasing
her. None of them seemed fast enough to catch her or strong
enough to hold her. At that moment she possessed incredible
strength. Hatti had just received word from the local police they
had terminated the four day search for her two boys, ages nine
and eleven who were missing, and presumed dead. There were
rumors. During the last four weeks, five black boys had

disappeared suddenly, nationally. Her sons were last seen in Prospect Park playing with other children. Now on this dull, fading afternoon neighbors chased Hatti down Bedford Avenue to stop her from committing suicide. Sebek was the first to grab hold of her. His restraint was ineffective for Hatti continued to run dragging him with her. She had snapped. For days she walked around hopeful that the police would find her children. When they called off the search, it suddenly hit her that her boys were really gone.

Neru and Khetnu were standing at the corner selling drugs in the neighborhood when they noticed Hatti, barefoot and running toward them. Both Khetnu and Neru's parents were civil servants who were hopeful that their sons would go to college. Khetnu's mother was a high school teacher and his father a fireman. Neru's mother was a social worker and his father a police officer. Khetnu and Neru begged their parents not to send them to college to be trained to work for someone else and make their employer wealthy.

Neru swore to his parents that he would rather die than slave nine to five making someone else's dream come true. "I ain't cut out for dat! I'd rather stand on the corner and sell drugs!" he told his parents.

Khetnu wanted to be a rapper and Neru was on his way to becoming a successful businessman as a street chemist. The first product he was marketing was nickel bags and rocks in Crown Heights, Brooklyn. But Sebek and the other elders in the community did not give up on them.

The boys, out of respect, would indulge their parents, and then go about their business of selling and hustling.

"Yo 'Ru, she snapped, y'all. Darn, I would a never thought she would snap! She seemed all together!" Khetnu was saying as the two walked toward the park on Sullivan Street. Neru lit a blunt and started to smoke. "Guess you are out of a customer!" Neru told him.

Khetnu sat back on the bench, and tilted his head backward. He dissected the smoke encircling his head as if for some hidden message. Finally a rhyme flowed out of his mouth:

> "Transcriptions of the afflicted.
> Her life was scripted
> By the 'most high.'
> Destined to uplift 'him' that dwells within her soul,
> Casualties of war with her life painted in diction.
> Embodied conviction in her intuition
> She soon realized that her gift is also her curse.
> She ran the streets to see a reflection of her soul.
> Combing her mind for locked thoughts and to her surprise,
> As she visualized herself being peaceful during adversities
> Her divinity became a reality!!!"

"Nice! Nice!" Neru encouraged him slapping high fives.

"Yo 'Ru cover me man, I am running to the crib. I'll be right back." Khetnu said jumping over the bench and disappearing through the gate.

"Why I always got to hold down the fort?" Neru shouted, chasing after him.

"I'll be right back. Give me twenty minutes." Khetnu told him.

"Ok! Ok! If you gonna leave me out here by myself at least let me hold Sweet Dreams." Neru bargained.

"Hell No! You can't have the Dream. Man, O'Jay finds out I loaned you Sweet Dreams, man I'll be one messed up brother! Besides, 'Ru you know you can't be trusted with a gun!" Khetnu countered.

"C'mon Khetnu, you can't leave me out here all by myself hanging like dat! You know if Junebug swing by he's gonna try to kill me. Dat boy don't have any love for me and you know dat!" Neru begged.

Sweet Dreams was the nine millimeter Khetnu carried in his waist. He saw Khetnu's hesitation.

"C'mon man, why you always forcing me into this antithetical and confrontational relationship. But you got a point, when dat boy swing by here and sees his mother crazed like that, no telling he might just start shooting up the hood." Neru again bargained.

"OK! I am gonna let you hold Sweet Dreams but a minute. I'll be right back. Please don't do anything stupid." Khetnu begged

Neru handing over Sweet Dreams. He then crossed Sullivan Street and headed up Washington Avenue feeling uneasy about leaving Sweet Dreams with Neru.

Neru spotted Ra Heru Khuti and Ifa Dare pulling up on Bedford Avenue and hustled over to the car.

"Yo, which one of you lil' punks sold her dat stuff?" Ifa Dare asked Neru.

"Don't be lookin' at me!" Neru sounded.

"It don't matter, when Junebug swings by, all you be dead for selling dat stuff to his mother. If I were you I'll be getting the hell outta dodge!" Ifa Dare told him.

"I ain't afraid of Junebug. He got all y'all wound up. But somebody got to step up and get bloody." Neru said reaching for Sweet Dreams.

"Oh Gawd! Who da fool gave you dat? Give it here." Ifa Dare said getting out the car.

"Yo' step off man, don't play with me like dat, unless you want to die." Neru said to him. Ra Heru Khuti got out the car and grabbed Ifa Dare's arm, pulling him back.

"Look at his eyes man! He's crazy enough to pop ya. Let him be!"

"Yea!" Neru urged, "Sedate yo' boy before I lay him out! I rule Bed Stuy, bro'. That's the difference between y'all and me. I ain't afraid of dat punk. Junebug done psych y'all out. He steps up to me, I'll get him! Word! Tell him stay off me! Yea, I represent Bedford crew. I know what yo' thinking but O'Jay got my back. Tell Junebug stay tha hell outta tha 'ford!" Neru said backing off on to the curb.

They were just getting back into the car when Sabu crossed the street and approached them. Sabu always traveled with his *Djuns Djuns* on his back. "Yo' why y'all messin' with dat crazy child? You know dat boy is ill!"

Sabu and Ra Heru Khuti went way back to high school. They both attended Boys and Girls High and were members of the track team. After graduation, Sabu went into the Army and Ra Heru Khuti went to Temple University. While in the service, Sabu visited a number of African countries and started playing the drums. After the service, he studied the drums full time. Fifteen years later, he had mastered at least twenty different types of drums from all over the continent. He retuned to the U.S. and started teaching a drumming class sponsored by the Music Department at Medgar Evers College in Brooklyn. Eight years ago, he met Damali and they had two babies but they never got married. One day he went to visit the children and the landlord told him Damali had taken the children and moved elsewhere. Sabu was shattered. He searched everywhere and could not find her. Finally, there was word that Damali had moved down south with her family to Alabama. Five years ago he married Kaheri Maat who also taught African dance classes at Medgar Evers College. Kaheri gave birth to two children, Sanu Pera, age four and Haiti Nu, age two. Sabu still nourished hopes of reconciliation with his first two children.

"Was it him that sold her bad drugs?" Sabu asked Ifa Dare indicting Neru.

"Ah don't know but there will be ass to pay when Junebug get up here!" Everyone referred to Junebug as Fifty Plus. By now a large crowd had gathered on Bedford Avenue. They had restrained Hatti to sitting on the curb. She was yelling at the police.

"Y'all know who killed my sons! Y'all know who killed my boys! America killed my boys. One of you killed my boys. The same one that's killing 'em black boys in Atlanta!" Recently, there were two incidents of black boys disappearing in Atlanta, Georgia and Detroit, Michigan. Hatti believed these disappearances were all connected. The neighbors were leading Hatti back to her apartment.

"Let's go to the Het. I promised Kaheri I'll meet her there," Sabu insisted.

"You go ahead. I have to take care of personal business. I'll catch up later," Ifa Dare told Ra Heru Khuti, stuffing a few rolls of hundred dollar bills in his pocket. Ra Heru Khuti could feel the weight of the rolls and knew Ifa Dare had put at least $50,000 in his pocket. Before he could object, Ifa Dare was heading back to the car. Ra Heru Khuti and Sabu headed down to down Bedford Avenue and crossed Empire Boulevard.

Chapter 14: Waters of Nu

Sanu Pera and Haiti Nu were playing on the pavement outside the Het Neter when they saw Sabu approaching and ran towards him. They entered the Het with Sanu Pera and Haiti Nu both clinging to their father's waist.

In the courtyard everyone was seated in a circle and dressed in white. The drummers were warming up. Neith sat in the front row with a few of her friends. Ra Heru Khuti glanced around and noticed the crowd was mostly women. The men sat in the back along with the drummers. Mut Kaheri and two other women were speaking to Sabu who was setting up with the rest of drummers. Ra Heru Khuti took a seat in the back with the rest of men.

Surrounding the courtyard was a beautiful garden, filled with all kinds of exotic flowers of all shapes and colors. In the southwest corner of the courtyard was a large fountain with cascades of water flowing among colorful lights. In front of the fountain was a large wooden table covered with yellow and green tie dyed cloth. The table was filled with dark chocolate covered strawberries, peaches, mangoes and orange slices sprinkled with cinnamon. The scent of sandalwood and honeysuckle caressed the light breeze that teased summer's evening, intoxicating the celebrants with each breath they breathed. The soft gentle sound of the drums invited arms and waists to twirl in harmony with it. The sounds of birds chirping melodiously in the air created a rhythm of their own and the festive soul singing sounds of Vam Klim Saugh in the background solicited effortless caresses and embraces. It seemed as if everyone had become one with each other. The women seemed to be flowing, the watery movements becoming the dance itself. Uninhibited, they moved their hips, twirling as if they had rehearsed all their lives for this moment.

"There is a revolution taking place," one of the sisters was saying softly into the microphone. Ra Heru Khuti could not tell who she was since the rest of the twirling sisters closely encircled her. She continued, "The Het Heru Healing Dance is part of that revolution. More and more women are turning away from Western approaches and they are returning to the tradition of their mothers, their grandmothers, the healing tradition of their ancestors. Once again we are called to bathe in the waters of the Nu, in the waters of the Mississippi, of the Nile, of the Yangtze, of the Amazon and the Essequibo rivers. Women are again learning how to use their own healing powers which are awakened through the power of movement and dance. Women in the past were their own doctors, nurses and midwives. They worked in harmony with the environment, utilizing herbs, gems, sounds and movement to balance their bodies and maintain a state of equilibrium. Today, the pharmaceutical companies send their scientists to remote locations in Africa, Asia, and South America to scout for plants that the ancients used effectively for healing purposes. Their findings are converted into billion dollar patents and profits for global capitalist companies and nothing for the people who shared this knowledge with them.

But there is one resource, which we possess that is free, accessible at all times and extremely effective. That is the healing force within you which when properly cultivated can move mountains, cause seas to overflow and nations to erupt. The Het Heru Healing Dance provides women with an effective means of healing the female reproductive organs, regulating their menstrual cycles, and promoting fertility. Het Heru, in the ancient Kamitic tradition, is the divine principle that symbolizes the imagination, the essence of beauty, attraction, grace, joy, creativity, inner peace, love and harmony. When these divine qualities are aroused and strengthened in women, then healing and harmony in social and marital relationships are promoted."

All the women were wrapped into one tight embrace, their hips swaying from side to side. As water was sprinkled over their bodies, the laughter of aroused giggles danced off their lips. "The

Het Heru Healing Dance fully synchronizes breathing, sound and movement to create a healing technology which is as effective today as it was thousands of years ago." At the end of the healing dance, Kaheri came over to Ra Heru Khuti and introduced him to Satra Maat, one of the sisters that was in the midst of the circle. From moment to moment through the crowd their eyes met, locked and separated. Satra Maat was tall, dark and wore a perpetual heavenly smile. Ra Heru Khuti knew he didn't have a chance as she danced her way over to him.

"Hetep!" Satra Maat greeted him. Kaheri was always meddling in his business, trying to get him married. But this was one time he didn't mind her meddling. He would have to thank her later.

"Hetep!" he said nervously. They exchanged numbers but Kaheri wanted more. She tore Satra Maat away from him and ushered her over to Shekhem-t Meter Ari for a reading. Ra Heru Khuti decided to walk to the front of the building while the priestess consulted the *Metu Neter* Oracle. Soon, he would know his fate. He was definitely interested in getting to know Satra Maat with the hopes of pursuing a relationship.

Outside, he stood next to the large tree that towered over the front of the building resisting the urge to lean against it. Sabu was crossing the street amidst the flow of the traffic. He paused midway across the street and was staring at something to his left. Ra Heru Khuti leaned lazily against the parking meter, waiting for Sabu to cross the street. His armpit felt wet and he dismissed it as the nervous sweat brought on by Satra Maat's smile. Intuitively, he glanced over his shoulder directly across the street.

There it was, the black Mercedes Benz slowly creeping up to him. Sabu, still walking, looked back at the car trying to see through the tinted windows. Instinctively, he ducked, using the tree as a shield. The driver stepped on the gas as the car sped toward Ra Heru Khuti with bullets spraying out of the window. The car then sped away burning tires as it turned on Lincoln Place.

Satra Maat and Kaheri were at Ra Heru Khuti's side assisting him to his feet. "What was that?" Satra Maat was saying, "Who was that?"

"I don't know!" Ra Heru Khuti lied as the Het's security guards gave chase. He had clearly seen Dante and Omawale in the car. He looked around for Sabu but he couldn't be found.

Dante was Sethe's special assistant. He was certain they grabbed Sabu. He couldn't risk his relationship with Saatra and Kaheri by telling them that Sabu had been abducted. In other words, Dante did all of Sethe's dirty work and was paid handsomely for it because if he was ever caught, Sethe was going to disavow any relationship with him. Before working with Sethe, Dante worked for the FBI as a field agent placed in New

York City's Municipal Government where he held several positions at various city agencies. His primary responsibility was to seek out subvergents working for the government. His last assignment was with the New York City Department of Pest Control where he was effective in harassing African Americans and Latino workers into leaving their jobs which were then given to young white males and females who no longer could find jobs in the private sector because of the budget cuts and a crumbling economy. His racism was so obvious that even the Commissioner of Pest Control had requested his reassignment, but to no avail. He came to work for Sethe as a special security assistant highly recommended by the Police Commissioner of Nassau County who was a personal friend of Sethe, it was rumored.

"You are bleeding!" Satra Maat exclaimed.

"You are shot!" Kaheri cried out loud.

"It is nothing! It's only a scratch." He told them, examining his arm. Ra Heru Khuti was puzzled. How did blood get under his armpit if he wasn't shot? He remembered feeling wet under his armpit but thought it was nervous sweat. A bullet had grazed his armpit.

"I am not hurt! I am not hurt!" Ra Heru Khuti was saying.

"Aren't you lucky?" Satra Maat said.

"He's not lucky! It's not his time yet!" Kaheri corrected her, tugging on her friend's sleeve.

"We have to go before we are late." She explained.

"Where y'all going?" Ra Heru Khuti said thinking of tagging along.

"We are trying to get some tickets for the boat ride," she said. Satra Maat was making signs at him, "Call me! Call me!" she begged.

Ra Heru Khuti felt flattered. He reached inside his pocket to make sure the paper with her number was there when Neith interrupted him.

"Who is she?" Neith asked with her arms folded across her stomach.

He had forgotten that Neith was there.

"I'm going to that boat ride and she had better not be on it!" Neith challenged him. "You are taking me!" she told him, looking straight into his eye.

"What boat ride?" Ra Heru Khuti asked.

"Oh please boy, don't play with me!" Neith told him.

He decided not to deny it. Obviously, she was in no playful mood. He also had a lot on his mind. He had to figure out a way to get Sabu back.

Chapter 15: Breast Ironing

Khetnu was still feeling uneasy about leaving Sweet Dreams with Neru. Khetnu's little sister Meri Ab was having a crisis. She was trying to convince her mother that it was inhumane for her to undergo the breast ironing ritual. But her mother was still insisting that Meri Ab go through the ritual.

"It's not humane." She protested.

"Almost every little girl in Cameroon who is oversized for her age goes through it at puberty. It's been happening for centuries, who are you to say this is inhumane?" Her mother argued.

"But this is not Cameroon! This is America!" Meri Ab pleaded.

"See! That's the problem, right there!" Her mother countered.

"Khetnu, please! Would you tell her, this is wrong!" Meri Ab pleaded to Khetnu.

"Yo! Why y'all getting' me involved in your female business!" Khetnu replied dryly. Meri Ab was determined not to go through with this ritual. Her pleas had convinced him to do some cursory research. He discovered that despite education campaigns by women's groups, about one-fourth of girls in Cameroon still undergo the "breast-ironing" ritual at puberty as their families attempt to squash their developing bosoms to make them sexually unattractive to boys and reduce their temptation to marry. The most popular "ironing" instrument is a heated wooded pestle, mashed painfully against the chest. Some girls are supportive of it because they claim it allows them to stay in school like other girls who have no breasts.

"Gee Meri Ab, you are kinda making a big thing out of this, aren't you?" Khetnu teased his little sister who had locked herself in her room, crying.

"Ok! Girl stop crying! You know I'm not going let anybody do anything that would hurt you! So relax!" he comforted her, as he thought of how he was going to convince his mother not to put her through the ritual.

There was loud banging on the door. Both Khetnu and Meri Ab ignored the loud racket. Soon their mother was yelling,

"Khetnu, get the door! You know it's only yo' crazy friends that bang on the door like that!" Khetnu grabbed his sneakers pushing past a distraught Meri Ab in the doorway and ran down to the door.

"Who dat?" He yelled.

"It's Sebek." The voice yelled back, "Yo man everybody is looking for you." Sebek told him. Khetnu opened the door and knew immediately something terrible had happened. Sebek was pale and rattled.

"Ok! Ok! Calm down, what happened?" Khetnu asked, nervously shaking Sebek to talk.

"Oh man! You ain't heard? Dat fool Neru shot Junebug! Don't know what's gonna happen now. Hatti done lost another son. She was half crazy. Now she full time crazy son – seven thirty! Sahu been texting and calling you! Where's yo' Blackberry?"

Khetnu ran back upstairs and grabbed his Blackberry phone off the bed. The phone was turned off because he had forgotten to recharge the battery.

"C'mon," Khetnu yelled at Sebek, running out the building and on to Washington Avenue. He crossed Sullivan Street, ran onto Montgomery Street and spotted Sahu on his cell leaning on his Jaguar. He saw Neru approaching. "Git yo' ass over here boy!" Sahu yelled at him closing the phone. "Who gave dat fool a piece? And why you not on point?" Sahu demanded.

Khetnu and Neru worked for Sahu. In fact, Sahu never wanted to hire Neru because he was reckless and it took a lot of convincing before Sahu reluctantly agreed. Sahu ran with low profile individuals. Neru was too hyper and he was on an early release program from Rikers Island Correctional Facility where he did one year of a two year sentence. He was on probation, pending no new arrests. Sahu promised them they both would be out of the business in two years. By all reasonable calculations, in two years they both would have made enough money for

Khetnu to start his own record label and get out of the drug selling business.

"I just went to take a crap! I left ten minutes ago to take a crap!" Khetnu yelled back.

"Why didn't you call it in?" Sahu screamed at him threatenly.

"Did he call it in?" Sahu asked Ras, his assistant.

"Not here!" Ras said.

"I just went to take a crap!" Khetnu defended himself.

"And who gave dat fool a piece?" Sahu asked. "The cops gonna be all up in here in a minute!" Sahu reasoned. "Give Ras yo' piece. You know how much dis is gonna cost me? I want everybody to lay low for a while 'til I say something," Sahu told Khetnu.

"Give it here!" Ras threatened Khetnu, holding out his hand.

"I left it with Neru for protection!" Khetnu nervously explained to him.

Both Ras and Sahu had terrible tempers. In an instant Sahu pulled out his nine millimeter and snatched Khetnu by the throat. "Fool! You did what?" He stuck the gun in Khetnu's mouth.

"Blow his damn head off!" Ras encouraged.

Khetnu's eyes were bulging out of their sockets. He had seen Sahu shoot many others because of a slight mistake. He knew what the man was capable of. Sahu lowered the gun

"Where dat fool at?" he asked Khetnu.

"I don't know! I left him on point!" Khetnu again explained.

Sahu turned to Ras. "Find him before the cops do and bring him to me. I'm gonna kill him myself." Sahu promised. He released the grip on Khetnu's throat.

"You better pray New York's finest finds dat fool before I do!" he told Khetnu driving off.

Khetnu knew Neru was in a whole lot of trouble, but he couldn't cut him loose. Neru had done favors for Khetnu. Khetnu was in debt to him. But carrying him was becoming a burden. He decided this was the defining line. After this, Khetnu decided, Neru is on his own. He had to think fast of a way to get Neru out of this mess and save his own head.

Chapter 16: King's Chamber

Anpu and Ras had sent word for Ra Heru Khuti to meet them at the printery. Ifa Dare and Sabu decided to ride along because they didn't like the sound of it. Ras and Anpu were sitting in front of the building as they pulled up in Ifa Dare's car.

Anpu invited them to sit down as he got right to the point. "I am an old man. I don't have much time to spare. Me and this building go way back. Before the house burned down and was abandoned by Sethe's father, the elder, I used to work here for him. He left the property to me and I built my dream–this printing press. There's lots of things you youngun's don't know. I tried to warn you when you found the book but you didn't listen. Sethe's old man kept all kinds of books, some good and some evil. I read most of them. Each night before I left, I would steal one book, take it home and read as much as I could and then bring it back the next day before anyone missed it. Sometimes, I would make copies of some pages. Sethe the elder never knew I could read so he would leave everything open in front of me."

Anpu cleared his throat and continued. "He thought I was so dumb, he would talk his business right in front of me. He could never imagine I was intelligent enough to make sense out of any of it. The reason why Sethe and Apep will kill you for that book is because their best plans are in limbo. Sethe's father made plans to replicate the King's Chamber right here in New York. When they were drafting the plans, the house burned down with everything in it. I knew all the books were burned except the ones I had stolen. But after you found that book, it re-ignited the idea of rebuilding the King's Chamber once more to the exact measurement that it was built in Khamit. Very powerful men in this nation have invested in the chamber, and they would stop at nothing to get their hands on that book. No one is safe!"

Anpu spoke deliberately, carefully choosing his words. "The *Oracle at Thebes* foretold of a time in the old kingdom when the Aryans sacked the land. This was witnessed with the coming of the age of Aries when Sethe and his followers who called themselves the master race, began pillaging the world."

Anpu continued, "Before that time the pyramid builders and the Shemsu Heru reigned in Kamit during the Age of Taurus around the year 2000 – 3000 BC. The skilled pyramid builders and the Shemsu Heru built the Great Pyramid of Giza. When the length of the day equaled the length of the night, the king sat in the King's Chamber as the star Sirius or Sept Tept was rising above the horizon. Through this chamber, a shaft was aligned directly to the pole star which is approximately aligned with the

Earth's axis of rotation at the equinox. The powerful light of the pole star would shine directly through upon the king – the Shekhem Ur Shekhem, who was seated under the shaft. When you are outside, all the stars are shining on you. But isolated in the King's Chamber, at specific times of year, nothing but the energy from that star passes through the shaft directly to the Shekhem Ur Shekhem. Why is it so important that Sethe and his followers want to replicate this exact setting to capture the energy from the stars? Did you know the radioactive waves from the stars have the power to knock the electrons out of atoms? These radioactive waves carry an intelligence code. The world's best kept secret is that all living things have as their foundation, electromagnetic and atomic forces behind them. In short, life is light." Anpu spoke with such conviction Ra Heru Khuti realized Anpu was more than what he pretended.

The more he spoke, the more Ra Heru Khenti realized, how ancient Anpu seemed. He continued. "It says here the Supreme Being placed the stars in the heavens to serve as markers of the destiny of men and the nations." Anpu's words were beginning to penetrate deep into Ra Heru Khuti's consciousness.

"Even before the sun and the Earth were created, the stars were placed in the heaven to serve as indicators of the destiny of men and the futurity of nations." Anpu carefully lit a cigar, took a puff and held the cigar between his three fingers. He spoke from behind the clouds of smoke.

"If you knew how to read the stars," he insisted in his mystical tone as his words captured their hearts, "You would know about the destiny of men. There is an ancient knowledge that the stars send out vibrations, radiations that affect your consciousness. Every vibration emits a sound. When a star is directly above, it has its greatest power upon you. Rising in the east, when the sun is directly above, is *Sirius Sept Tept*, which is the star that corresponds to the light, the guiding light of the east, the Eastern Star, or the star that corresponds to the eastern horizon of heaven." Anpu paused, took another puff of the cigar, filling the room with smoke as he exhaled.

Ra Heru Khuti silently focused on how he would keep the papyrus concealed even from Anpu and Ras.

"What I am saying is Sirius, the Dog Star, is the closest star to our sun. Have you ever heard of the Dogons? The Dogons, several hundred years ago, told that there are two other stars that are part of the Sirius Star system. They call them the *Pup Stars* – the two companions. The force of gravity is so strong they have collapsed within themselves and retain light. They're not reflecting out, so you can't see them with the naked eye-unless, of course, you understand the words written in the *Papyrus Am Tuat*." Again Anpu paused and took another puff on the cigar and continued to tap the table with the huge ring he wore on his index finger. He seemed distant and he smiled, showing his large teeth, stained yellow from smoking.

"Of course, you can't see them, because they're not emitting light. Light does not bounce off them, because light gets absorbed through the heavy gravitational pull. All stars emit sound. The radio telescopes that were aimed at Sirius began to pick up positive energy and these interferences move in an orderly manner. Tracking the movement over a period of time, Sethe and his confederates were able to calculate where the movement would take place in another ten years. They plotted the exact coordinates for the King's Chamber." Anpu's big teeth glistened behind the cloud of smoke.

Occasionally, Anpu would break into hysterical laughter, almost uncontrollable, and drips of saliva would slide down his lips. His laughter brought on more laughter. Soon Ra Heru Khuti was laughing besides himself. It all seemed funny. This time Ra Heru Khuti noticed that the ring Anpu was tapping the table with was emitting yellow beams of light.

"They predicted the orbit Sirius follows. The length of the orbit was sixty years. Every sixty years, Sethe and his confederates have a major ceremony to mark when the star completed its orbit." Anpu said.

Ras laughed so loudly he could not restrain himself, and he joined in the conversation. "Sethe and his confederates claim to travel to these stars in their astral bodies," Ras interjected.

Anpu, not to be undone, took control of the conversation. "Sethe and his followers have been after that power for hundreds of years. Now they are at the brink of regaining that power because the exact coordinates of the King's Chamber is in the *Papyrus Am Tuat* which you have Ra Heru Khuti. Inscribed inside the *Papyrus Am Tuat* are the actual dimensions of the size of the Earth, the distance from the Earth to the sun, and many other fundamental calculations and measurements."

The beam of light emitting from Anpu's ring changed from yellow to red. Ra Heru Khuti felt his heartbeat increase. His eyes were transfixed on the red beam coming from Anpu's ring. Ras was still chatting.

"I tell you all this because I want you to understand the magnitude of what the Sethe family is trying to accomplish. I want you to comprehend that the events that have been set in motion are larger than you and are strongly influenced by the stars."

Ra Heru Khuti no longer knew fear because his mother's words resounded throughout his body and he chose to convey this message to both Anpu and Ras. He knew it was his destiny to lead the Shemsu Heru to protect the *Papyrus Am Tuat*. "I come from a tradition of using the stars in a positive way. I too have been a star rider. You don't scare me!" Ra Heru Khuti told Anpu who seemed unaffected by his words.

"Sethe believes he could convince you to help him replicate the interior structure of the inner chamber with perfect alignment. For this you will be rewarded well. Sethe controls some very powerful and wealthy men in America. Sethe's astrological sign is Virgo which is directly opposite the constellation of Pisces and is ruled by Mercury which governs commerce, commercialism, money and business-the foundation of the Sethian empire."

"The *Papyrus Am Tuat* contains not only a draft of the design of the King's Chamber of the Pyramid of Giza but perhaps most importantly, the eleven laws of Maat and the words of power to convert the star's light into spiritual power. That's why Sethe would kill for that book. Give it up to Sethe before it costs you your life." Anpu warned Ra Heru Khuti.

Anpu and Ras stood up together; both men towered over Ra Heru Khuti. Anpu aimed the beam of light from his ring straight toward Ra Heru Khuti's heart. Ra Heru Khuti felt dazed and dizzy. He felt he was losing control over his senses as the red light penetrated into his heart.

"Give it to him before it's too late. Give it to him and go on the boat ride and enjoy yourself." Anpu repeated moving the ring closer to Ra Heru Khuti's heart. Ras climbed over the table and was directing his middle finger into the center of his chest. Ra Heru Khuti felt his energy fading as he gasped for air. The beam of light was draining his energy.

Chapter 17: Stepping off the Balcony

Bast and Sekhet were sisters and they were more closely linked than most people imagined. Their friendship extended beyond incarnations. The two women laughed happily as they held hands and ran alongside the walls in the courtyard. Sunlight suddenly shone on their copper toned bodies from above. White linen dresses hung loosely on their bodies, not revealing their perfect curves. They both knew they were under the watchful eyes of the men who worked in the courtyard.

Their playful giggles resounded as the wind took their laughter and spread it out of the courtyard, into the fields, and up the mountains. They ran toward the approaching figure of their favorite cousin. His outline was shadowed by the shining sun, and his clothes blew in the wind. With each step he came closer to them, causing their hearts to beat faster and their giggles to grow louder. Bast flung her arms out to embrace him as she out ran Sekhet, her hair flowing in the wind. Sekhet, the more reserved of the two, took her time walking to greet the golden figure. Bast strolled beside her cousin, Ra Heru Khuti, as Sekhet lagged behind.

The street market was in full swing outside the courtyard on the main street. South Fourth Street was closed to all vehicles, with the exception of pony rides, and antique cars for viewing only. There were amazing spectacles of belly dancers, musical attractions, and the aroma from the food tables laden with everything imaginable, from sweet mesquite grilled barbecued tofu to cumin and chile pepper infused tacos. Shopping the South Fourth Street fair is as exciting as traveling to New York City's Thirty-Fourth Street metropolis. The stores may be the same as those in any country but the tastes and products are different. Shoppers can find some of the best deals in designer clothing with matching bags, fur and jewelry. Every year, around this time, South Fourth Street becomes the fashion capital where people don't get tired of being fabulous. The designer shops that line both sides of the street gladly display discount signs of up to ninety percent. Bast eyed a chandelier created from a cow yoke, a pair of French chairs, and a nesting group of tables that were eagerly purchased by one of the fair enthusiasts. Folks moving around the street fair could sip cocktails or red wine, as well as partake of grapes and canapés against a backdrop of blooming flora and hundreds of craft vendors and artisans.

One of the vendors in the market featured a pet-portrait artist in front of her boutique. The artist presented "optical traveling art pieces," that were original and intriguing. She is one of those very talented South Fourth Street artists who can paint your cat's portrait as well as "faux" your walls – or "trellis" them. Another popular hangout was Lars Bolander Ltd., where Bolander, himself, was in the store with many friends and admirers, showing off lots of beautiful accessories, including those big mushrooms, made of wood in France.

The highlight of the festival each year is the "Taste" featuring several of the low country's favorite restaurants offering patrons a chance to sample appetizers, main courses and desserts from their menu, all for one dollar each.

Bast and Sekhet changed direction and headed down a side street. Both of them were veteran shoppers and knew the less expensive shops with just as many designer names were located in the backstreets. They were met by a group of youth in baggy jeans, gold necklaces, giant baseball caps and oversized T-shirts, and young, blond women wearing short skirts and high heels. They formed a circle and took turns dancing in the center. Limbs were flying in every direction or even writhing and spinning to the beat of the music as they performed dance moves that seemed to say, "You got served" to the other participants.

As they ran out onto the side street Bast heard a voice talking. It wasn't from the outside. It wasn't anyone on the street or sidewalk or in a yard. The voice was distinct above the chattering and noise from the street fair, vendors and tourists.

The voice spoke in an archaic Egyptian language and it came from inside the building to their left. It was obvious that no one else had heard the voice. The words or phrases at first sounded like gibberish but Bast soon realized it was an ancient language spoken by Egyptians during the Old Kingdom. Bast had taken enough ancient Semitic and Hamitic languages to realize that this person - this voice, this whoever or whatever it was - was speaking an ancient language of Egypt. She recognized a few words, but couldn't translate any more than that. She continued to look around to see if anyone would materialize. No one ever did. The voice was so compelling that it caused her to stop and stare at the building from whence it came.

"What is it?" Ra Heru Khuti asked, holding his cousin's cold hands.

"She gets this way sometimes." Sekhet tried to explain to Ra Heru Khuti. Then as if to answer his question, a woman appeared on the balcony of the building from whence the voice came. She stood on the balcony towering over them, her hair and white dress flowing loosely in the wind. Her face stared straight ahead, never looking down. She walked on to the fire escape and stepped off the balcony as if she was walking on solid ground. She stepped off the balcony, left foot first, and fell to her death holding a book with blank pages in her hand. She fell from the eleventh floor without any struggle or fear. She freely surrendered herself to death. Her body flowed through the air until it landed on the north side of the building, in the street. Bast stood in awe holding Ra Heru Khuti's hand when there suddenly appeared two imposing figures on the same balcony from which the woman had fallen. The two figures looked down and directly at them.

"Let's go!" Ra Heru Khuti screamed at them as Bast and Sekhet gazed up at the imposing figures staring down at them. They recognized the two figures as Sethe and Apep.

Chapter 18: Mastery Over the Ka

At home Bast fled to her bedroom, threw herself on the bed, clasped her face into her hands and wept. Her two favorite cats, Raat and Temt, sat high up in her bedroom windowsill. The cats seemed totally confused by her present state. Bast liked her room because of the acoustic mettle.

This particular "home-away from home" was perched on a hillside overlooking a ravine. The five-story house, with undulating walls of wood and floor-to-ceiling glass windows with an extraordinary view seemed like the perfect hide away. Her parents had constructed this house to get away from the outside world, and to cherish privacy and seclusion. She pushed a button and a twenty-four foot wall of glass windows vanished into the floor, revealing the pool area outside.

Since she was expecting friends for dinner, Bast rambled around in the kitchen, marinating some gluten chunks and tossing chopped leeks, red peppers and corn in a deep soup pot to simmer. Cooking certainly took her mind away from the tragedy she had just witnessed. Meanwhile, Ra Heru Khuti made a fire in the fireplace to set the ambiance for the night.

"No more thoughts or mention of it," she chided herself. "Just focus on preparing dinner and what to wear," she thought. Sekhet helped Bast neatly arrange a party platter full of marinated tofu slices, raw vegetables, and a homemade mango salsa with cilantro. Then Bast ran back up the stairs to her room and stood in front of the full length mirror. She fanned out her arms, veiled in chiffon. She turned her body, swaying back and forth, raising her arms and twisting her hips as if she was modeling. The fabric flowed like a curtain, shielding her from prying eyes. She pretended she was performing before an enchanted audience in her living room where she sang and seduced them by her come-hither, keep-back performance. After preparing herself for her audience by practicing in the mirror, she made her way down the stairs to greet her arriving guests.

The dinner party was an interesting mix of people. Music was playing, sweet oils burning, the aroma of food cooking, colorful dim lights filled the living room and the fireplace created shadows of bodies swaying and twirling on the marbled floor. Faces turned to watch Bast glide into the room. Somewhere in the background someone was shaking a tambourine in tune to her steps.

Bast's stylistic persona was as rock steady as her clothing. She considered herself part healer and part juju woman. She regularly performed a one woman show called, "Heal a Woman: Heal a

Nation" where she mixed smooth movements with breathing and vibrating mantra sounds that brought her audience through an electrifying experience. At twenty-six, she was still working the gossamer tunics and shawls that influenced and gave her designs the feel of ritual and magic. Her closet still retained many of the fringed shawls and musky fragrances in homage to her lover whom she remembered spooning while wrapped in Nicksian feathers, leather and lace. Variations on her costumes were precursors of that grungy girl who wore the little ballerina dresses and big cowboy boots. She remembered her mother, adorned in her west coast Ophelia look, all ruffles and belled sleeves.

Standing in the middle of the room filled with intriguing guests, she felt her loneliness engulfing her thoughts. "I need a man," she smiled. "One that wouldn't mind the way I dress." She surrendered recalling one of her favorite outfits: a Jantzen leotard, a little chiffon wrap blouse, a little short jacket, skirt and boots. She reminisced over her wardrobe that encompassed the shaky vicissitudes of her romantic life.

"I didn't want to be held down by a relationship," she whispered, elaborating only that she was simply not equipped for the responsibilities of family life. Her one woman act served as a healing mechanism for her as well as her audience. Her assiduously cultivated mysteriousness helped to keep her alive in the minds of admirers. Yet, at times, she appeared guileless. Leaning in confidentially, she bemoaned the state of her arms.

"They'll never be what they were." She mused. To tone them, she flexed a few times a week on her Power Flex machine. She was limber enough, though, to lay out on the stage three variations of her favorite seductive dances. One of her dances featured a cutaway jacket, a ruche and ruffled dress, and chunky boots. Missing was the airy shawl-part of her personality.

"A shawl is a great prop," she mused, "it makes for big gestures." She spread her arms and whirled like a gyroscope that reached beyond the ocean and extended from her windows, giving her the feeling of a sorceress as she silently sang "Klim Saugh… Saugh…Saugh…" Dipping her pinky in her glass of nectar and rubbing it against her lips, she scolded herself. "C'mon girl! Stay focused, all your guests are watching your every move!"

The living room was beginning to fill with men dressed in Nicks-style top hats, and urbane looking women in black chiffon blouse's, sparkling crystal and brass filigree crescent moon pendants. Around the pool area Ra Heru Khuti was engaged in conversation with a group of tattooed bikers, basketball players and graffiti artists posing in a collection of hoodies, sweatpants, T-shirts and sweaters. A few of them sported thick black eye lashes and stitches for extra menace. Most of them were his friends.

Bast's eyes caught the figure of a tall man who rather than entering the room by walking through the door did a pommel-horse-style run-up the stairs, climbed onto oversize blocks, somersault and assumed a cross-legged seated position in the center of the room. A broad smile covered his face as he turned his gaze upward at Bast. She felt the power of his stare upon her. A heavy, oppressive energy immobilized her and before she knew it, in two giant successive leaps, he floated through the air and landed in front of her. She recoiled, alarmed by his sudden power and guile.

"Where is my manuscript?" he queried, grabbing her hand and cutting off her breathing. His hands were strong, muscular and smelled of blood. His palms generated such tremendous power. She felt her breath being dragged out of her and in her effort to retain her breathing she countered by bringing her knee to his groin as hard as she could. It had no effect on him. He merely laughed, feeling her knee against his crotch. Panicking, she kicked again frantically at his crotch, feeling her strength waning. Bast realized her hand was in the grip of Ap's power

"Tell me!" He insisted, "or I'll drain the life out of you!" The room was spinning. The lights were fading. The sounds of "Klim Saugh...Saugh...Saugh..." rang, tingling in her ears.

"Let her go!" Sekhet commanded, summoning and focusing her Ra force energy in the palms her hands. The pupils of her eyes became full and enlarged as she directed her life powers straight to Ap's heart. Without warning Sekhet grew into a brilliant ball of light. Ap gasped in pain and threw Bast, shattering the glass window she landed on. Sekhet, the light bearer, summoned Raat and Temt who were growling anxiously as Ap attacked Bast. The two cats sprang swiftly into the air; attacking Ap. Raat swung her claws into his right eye and scratched at his pupils, damaging his lens. Temt ripped into his face, tearing at his jaws. Ap, covering his damaged eyes, flung the cats away from him as he defended himself. Both cats hit the wall and fell on their feet as they pondered the damage they had done. Ap staggered for his footing, with blood oozing out of his right eye.

Without hesitation, Sekhet jumped on Ap cutting and hacking his head from his neck with her laser-like beams of light. She tore out his intestines and kicked them into the fireplace with her left leg and burned her name into his body with her beams of light, driving his soul from his body. Then, by making sounds unheard by the human ear, she dragged his life-force out of his body and obtained mastery over his body-Ka.

Bast lay coiled on the floor in blood. Astounded, Bast had never seen this side of her big sister who was slowly resuming her human form. Sekhet was covered in a dimming red and blue light, her voice unfamiliar. The fire in her eyes still blazed into what remained of Ap. Bast picked herself up off the floor and staggered over to Sekhet. As she reached for her sister's hand, Sekhet's cool glow encircled Bast and she began spinning in a spiral dance. She felt her body regaining strength as she flowed with inspired movements. She enjoyed a peaceful bliss for the first time, moist and harmonious, essentially hers. The excitement of her movements brought on such electric pleasure she felt as if she had danced out of her body and into an ecstatic consciousness of joy!

"This is the power of the Het Heru Clan!" Sekhet explained to her little sister who was still twirling around uncontrollably. "The power to lift consciousness above pain and suffering! Saugh…Saugh…Saugh, Tema Meri Hur Hetep, my little sister!" Sekhet, in the land of her ancestors, summoned the peace and joy required to walk with them. She spoke out of the distant places, for her physical form could not be seen.

"Tua – thanks for the peace and joy that comes from knowing who I am! Meri! Love! Meri! Love!" Sekhet sang as the ancient words penetrated the air.

"I have no enemies! I know no transgressors for I am El Shaddai!" With those words her image reappeared. She was dressed in white cloth and water dripped from her fingers.

Someone held a burning white candle behind her and sprinkled white rose petals on the floor of the room as if they had fallen out of the air. Her face appeared covered with white powder.

"I am magic!" Sekhet told Bast. "Embrace me and join our ancestors! Feel the fire! We will always protect you! En Aungkh Heh!" she whispered as she embraced Bast.

Chapter 19: Baby-Mama Drama

She remembered him fondly enough, seeing how she referred to him as "Mr. Slick." They met in a breakfast joint. She was standing next to him in line waiting to be seated. The waitress inquired if they were together. He said, "Not yet," and asked for her cell phone number. She gave him the digits. He programmed it in his trio, and called about a week later to arrange their first date. Their chance meeting blossomed from cell phone flirtation, to live-in relationship, to threatening phone calls, stalking outside the barbershop, and ultimately baby-mama drama. She accused him of sleeping with other women after tracking photos and calls on his phone, and he accused her of not trusting him.

Over the last five years Nephthys received welfare checks and food stamps. She was in a welfare-to-work program, and briefly held several jobs. In that time she also gave birth to her second and third child. Now, at age twenty, with a tenth grade education, Nephthys, was finally overwhelmed by the demands of work and family. So, in the winter, she showed up at the People's Emergency Center with three children, a fourth on the way, no job and no place to live.

Nephthys's life was simply too troubled by disabilities, turmoil and often bad personal choices. Poor education, lack of support from her family members, mental and drug problems, and unstable living conditions are common among Nephthys and her "hang out crew." She grew up with her brothers, a sister and a mother who split from her father early on. The family ended up on welfare. After Nephthys became pregnant in the tenth grade and dropped out of school, she continued living in the crowded, tumultuous house with her babies until last winter when her mother moved to a smaller home with two sons, her other daughter and that daughters two children.

The father of Nephthys's six year old son was out of the picture, and also fathered a daughter whose birth was imminent. The father of the three year old girl and her twenty-one month old boy was in prison. After the birth of the first child, she worked at Mc Donald's for several months. She could not stand it when one of the young boys that worked there referred to her as "Mom." She went into a jobs program, working twenty hours a week at a Young Women's Christian Association with her wages paid by the welfare office. She spent an additional ten hours a week in a required search for a permanent work program. Eventually she landed a receptionist job at a funeral home where she worked for several months. For the last two years Nephthys received cash welfare benefits of about five hundred dollars a month, plus about four hundred dollars a month in food stamps. She vowed not to have any more children and to get her General Education Diploma.

Nephthys and her children shared a two bedroom apartment with her younger brother Neru. Lately Neru had been staying at his new girlfriend's place. Neru came around to check on Nephthys and drop some "bills" on her. Although Nephthys appreciated the cash, she hoped that everything worked out between Neru and his girl so she and her kids could have the home to themselves.

Neru told her he met his girl Khatrasaim at a club in Manhattan. His buddy who worked as a doorman for Club Harveys invited him to the club and he met Khatrasaim there. Khatrasaim was impressed with Neru. He was handsome and broad shouldered. He spoke in a deep baritone voice and sported long dreadlocks and a goatee. He was three years older than Khatrasaim. Khatrasaim was with her girlfriend Aqmeri who kept pushing her on to Neru.

"Girl," she threatened, "if you don't grab him, I will! So you better make up your mind quick. That man is too damn fine to go to waste!" They both laughed as Aqmeri hugged Neru, giving Khatrasaim the eye. Khatrasaim and Neru didn't spend much time that night because Aqmeri kept interrupting.

Neru was smitten. If anything, he knew Khatrasaim was out of his league and he was determined to make her his. The following weekend they met again at Harveys and later that evening he made his move. They danced all night, closed down the club and Neru brought Khatrasaim back to her place. They next day Neru surprised her when he pulled up in front of her workplace in his rented Mercedes Benz Gl. He took her shopping and spent over five thousand dollars on clothes, shoes, bags and jewelry.

Khatrasaim loved the attention and the shopping sprees. That summer after daily walks in the park and weekend dinners, the couple moved in together at Khatrasaim's apartment.

Chapter 20: Mama Ayala's Black Stuff

Ra Heru Khuti carried Amseth's bleeding body into Mama Ayala's home. Mama Ayala was famous for her "black stuff" that seemed to heal all injuries, including strained muscles and pinched nerves. Because of her ailing health, many feared that the healing techniques passed down through generations of her family might be lost.

Mama Ayala referred to herself as a folk healer. Ask Mama Ayala, and she would tell you she was simply a woman who did what she could to heal sick neighbors, fueled largely by her knowledge of the healing powers of Auset. Auset is an ancient Egyptian goddess Mama Ayala studied. She learned about Auset's charms, enchantments, the art of choosing different healing leaves and botanical remedies.

Mama Ayala's roots traced back to Nigeria via New Orleans with strong ties to the *Bakus,* a people with strong spiritual attributes who are reputed to hold off thunder and lightning, attract rain, protect crops, cure people and defy gravity with

their mind altering ability. She was married to a folk healer in
New Orleans and gave birth to two young children when she had
to uproot herself, left New Orleans and relocated to New York.
To avoid her husband whom many in the Bayou called "the
African" doing harm to her children she gave them up for
adoption to her sister but kept close eyes on them. Mama Ayala
settled in Brooklyn, bringing her healing business with her.

Mama Ayala's techniques allegedly healed an array of minor
pains and injuries, such as pinched nerves, strained muscles and
sprains. More serious problems, such as broken bones, could be
cured by her massage treatment, she claimed.

Mama Ayala also specialized in stomach remedies – that's
where the "black stuff" comes in. In the same wooden box her
father hand made more than seven decades ago, Mama Ayala
kept a stained wooden bowl and thick masher. She used them to
grind the herbs *Obeah Bush*, *Monkey Ladder* and *Kapadula* into
a black paste. Then she mixed it with more of her secret powered
herbs and burned it, creating what she called an ugly, ugly
tasting, jet black concoction. She fed patients one spoonful of the
foul-smelling liquid and then massaged it through the stomach.
Obviously, it was not a method endorsed by modern medicine,
but Mama Ayala 's patients over the years attested to its potency.
A hat rack adorned with more than twenty brightly covered
rosaries hung in Mama Ayala's bedroom. Patients had donated

the gifts as thanks over the years. Mama Ayala, a woman of faith, said Auset gives her much healing power, and she did not charge people when she helped them.

She knew from the wild banging on her door that another emergency had arrived. A quick look at Amseth and Mama Ayala knew she had to bring her best medicine to work.

"The po' child look like a car wreck!" she thought to herself. Then she asked Ra Heru Khuti, "What happened?" after examining her. Amseth was badly cut and bruised above the forehead and scalp. She also had injuries on her shoulder, back, arms and legs. The severity of her injuries made Mama Ayala suspect a crime scene. Mama Ayala worked on Amseth round the clock, stitching, putting back together deep lacerations. She feared some of the injuries would cause permanent nerve damage but it was too soon to tell from the swellings on her patient's body.

Around four in the morning Mama Ayala took a break to wait for all of the swellings and soreness to decrease. To Amseth, the room was still spinning in circles as she felt dizzy and experienced loud headaches with no feelings on her forehead. She writhed in pain and longed for Mama Ayala to return to the room. Somehow Mama Ayala brought her peace and comfort despite her situation. Mama Ayala was gentle. Not that Amseth couldn't stand pain. In fact she was a firm believer in the old adage "no pain, no gain." With Mama Ayala out of the room she tried wiggling her eyebrows. It hurt but she was beginning to get feeling and movement in the face and head. Somehow, she managed to open and close her eyes.

When Mama Ayala returned again, Amseth noticed she had changed her clothing. She wore an ocean blue and white niong ting dress and her head was wrapped in the same blue and white niong ting. Pearl beads and a jade necklace dangled from her neck and her wrists. Softly Mama Ayala sang a chant she remembered that her mother often sang to her as a little girl. The old woman chanted as she began to apply the needles with such gentleness, Amseth barely felt anything. Once the needles were inserted into her face, neck and head, she felt very relaxed and even fell asleep.

When Amseth awoke, Mama Ayala was still working on her shoulder and arms. Mama Ayala placed her hand under the shoulder and tried to rotate it. Even asleep Amseth was hesitant because it hurt to move that arm. Mama Ayala continued to rotate the shoulder as she began to manipulate one of the needles. As quickly as she maneuvered the needle, Amseth instantly felt relief from the pain and regained total movement of her shoulder. When the animal threw her across the room, her feet slipped from under her, and she fell injuring her back. Movement of her torso was excruciating, and the pain traveled down the side of her right leg and around into her groin and down the inside of her leg. Amseth was so relaxed that she wasn't sure if she was asleep or in a daze because right there in front of her stood her son Ra Heru Khuti in brilliant form.

Ra Heru Khuti came to her, it seemed, in a dream and touched her body. As the needles were inserted into her back she sank into a deep relaxation. She watched Ra Heru Khuti as he extended his energy into her and she could feel the energy moving through her joints, fingers, wrists, shoulder and knees. She experienced a completely wonderful and relaxing feeling, soothing her muscles right down her spine. It was as if he was dancing and his movements were subtle and soft. Ra Heru Khuti's leg was bent over his whole body as he pushed upward. He was very acrobatic and each movement generated a surge of energy inside of her. His arm swooped down to his legs and then slowly back up to his chest. His whole body moved to the right, with his left leg empty, his left foot turned, body following, then right foot heel up turned, the arm was moving to the abdomen, palms were moving up staying with the abdomen then lower than the navel. His head moved slowly followed by his arms, hands, and then fingers. He bathed his body with the energy emanating from his palms. Then his arms and hands extended over his head as they swayed in rhythmic motion. Finally, the movements subsided and his hands came together and rested on Amseth's abdomen.

At that moment Mama Ayala reached into her bag and pulled out the "black stuff," her special blend of herbal medicine. She injected some of the "black stuff." Her head tilted backward as she twirled a few times around the room and blew a mouthful of the herbs into the air. Immediately, the room lit up with sparkling vapors. She fell on the chair in deep trance. After a few minutes, she opened her eyes, took some more of the "black stuff," chewed on it, and placed it on Amseth's cuts and bruises. She also applied some to the tip of the needles in Amseth's head and neck and lit a match to them. Ra Heru Khuti's dance had put her in a daze. The aroma from the medicinal herbs brewing in the ceramic pot was so intoxicating that within a few minutes she fell fast asleep.

In her sleep Amseth heard Mama Ayala chanting as her fingers began working the many areas of stagnation where she hemorrhaged, areas on her body which felt harder and more resistant to her touch. In other areas of her body she felt Mama Ayala's hand sinking deeper and deeper without any sense of substance within the area. She felt as if someone was looking straight through her. Her right side was more sensitive to touch and required more work than the left. Mama Ayala stood at Amseths' waist pressing down the channel, creating a circuit with her mother hand on the deficient areas and her son hand on the areas of excess. She continued to do this whenever she came across stagnant areas and worked around Amseth's upper body applying pulling techniques and pressing with the arms in different positions.

Mama Ayala also took the opportunity to work on the shoulders and discovered lots of tension. She continued pressing on the shoulders and upper back for a few minutes until the areas of tension felt softer. She then looked down Amseth's body and like magic her scapula was relaxed and sunk into the musculature of her back. She went down to her lower back, gluteus, thighs and calves, most of which felt restricted, and Amseth moaned because they felt sore and tender.

Then Mama Ayala turned her over onto her back and placed her hands gently on her abdomen, just leaving them there for a few minutes. When Amseth's breathing seemed to become more relaxed and natural, Mama Ayala gently pressed and rocked in small circles. Mama Ayala could feel that one of her hips was slightly higher than the other and continued to do more pressing, stretching, pulling and rolling techniques for the ankles, knees and hips. Amseth heard some sounds of crackling and crepidus coming from her knees and ankles, but they didn't seem to bother her. Mama Ayala asked her to get up and surprisingly to Amseth she was able to stand on her feet.

Mama Ayala reached for her head, turning her head from side to side. Then she started to spin her in circles. Amseth felt herself spinning and twirling uncontrollably. She wanted to stop but could not stop. She felt she was going to hurt herself but still could not stop. Then she stopped fighting against her twirling body and relaxed, giving into the spins and twirls. She could not see Mama Ayala nor Ra Heru Khuti anymore and her body kept spinning as if suspended by her head. She felt herself growing, getting bigger and bigger until she spun out into the galaxy. It was there that she stopped for a second and reached for a sparkling star and tucked it into her bosom. The healing ritual of *Aum Tam* had restored her health.

Then Amseth heard Mama Ayala beg Ra Heru Khuti, "Please! I beg of you! Save my boy! He is a good child! His father did this to him! I cannot fix him. His father is too powerful even in death! You must help him!" she continued to plead with him.

Chapter 21: Collision

Neru's increasingly violent behavior may have resulted in his psychotic breakdown. He felt tired of running and decided to commit suicide. He remembered the scene of unspeakable horror as he shot Junebug who had pushed him too far and he slapped Khatrasaim whom he no longer trusted. He couldn't understand why the crowd that poured in from around the area wanted him dead. Then there was the singing by some Gospel Choir, poetry by some uniformed youths and the release of the doves.

The news media made Neru out to be a senseless killer. He was profiled as an at-large parolee whom police linked to two deaths; Junebug and Khatrasaim. There was mad tension between Junebug and himself for quite some time and no one took his side. But the scene was played out several times in his head. Most people saw the shooting as playing into an oft-repeated narrative of a city rocked by runaway violence, where tensions between gang members and police run high and, all too often, boil over.

He contemplated slashing his wrists and stabbing himself in the chest shortly before parking his Jeep Cherokee on the tracks of a commuter railway line. He sat in the middle of the tracks and watched the two high speed trains approaching each other. The powerful lights from the trains exerted an unusual gravitational pull on his spirit. He stared at the light and felt peace and absolution from his murderous deeds.

It was then that he realized the light he was staring into was coming not from the trains but from another direction. It was a circulating light beam emanating from a ring laser. The circulating beam of light pulled him out of his jeep and dragged him effortlessly into a closed time-like loop. He stirred in empty space. Space and time became connected. Matter desecrated. He flowed in the crystal loop and consciously saw the two trains collide and derail in a fiery wreck. As the trains collided, he was still stirring in crystal light, as the optical fibers produced a path that formed a light cylinder. Neru raised his hand and dragged particles of a circulating light cylinder that became strong enough to form a circle in space which turned into a circle in time. Reversing the time sequence, he pulled the trains apart before they collided. He was a guest to witness a fluke of nature or the transparency of semitransparent beam splitters.

Why was he drawn into the realm of fiber optics, lasers, and vacuum chambers? Why was he given special ability to teleport out of the Jeep and stand on the side and watch the massive tragedy as the trains collided? Was this a payment for his crime?

The circulating light beam emanating from a ring laser engulfed him, shooting the two colliding trains toward him as he sat in his Cherokee. The loops closed and he stirred effortlessly in empty space.

One commuter train was southward bound. The second was traveling north toward the suburb of Moorpark. The collision — at six in the morning local time — happened in the northern Hills of Punt.

Both trains were derailed. Some carriages overturned, sending passengers tumbling down the aisles. In light rain, almost three hundred firefighters picked through twisted wreckage and carried wounded passengers to a nearby car park, where thirty-five ambulances were waiting to ferry them to hospitals. Rescuers used ladders to climb up to the windows of carriages lying on their side. Firefighters found bleeding passengers walking dazed amidst twisted wreckage and scattered belongings. Some survivors pushed others in shopping trolleys from a nearby shop. Emergency crews worked desperately through the night and into Saturday morning, ripping into the mangled train cars to search for an unknown number of trapped people. The death toll was expected to increase as firefighters dug deeper into the wreckage. The engine of the Union Pacific freighter was left on its side, its nose against the Metrolink wreckage. The rest of the freight train was mangled behind it.

Neru heard screams of agony as he ran through a smoky haze toward a wrecked train where dozens of bloodied passengers were still trapped inside. He pulled victims out one by one, some weeping as they looked about at the destruction. He worked on top of the wreckage and through breaches in the passenger car to reach dazed and injured victims.

The crash happened in an area where the tracks form a "U" shape, about as wide as a football field. At the top of the bend is a five hundred-foot long tunnel that runs beneath the train line. On the north side of the tunnel, there is a siding, a length of track where one train can wait for another to pass. It was from here that the gunmen ambushed four cops, spraying their vehicles with gunfire and rocket-propelled grenades. Four policemen were killed in the attack which occurred at the same time of the train crash.

Neru sat quietly leaning against the train wreck, his head down but not there. His left arm with the bone protuding out of the flesh hung limply on his dislocated shoulder. He scratched at the bleeding scars all over his body. He had broken bones, internal cuts, a torn cornea and burns over a tenth of his body. Worst was the head wound that kept him in and out of consciousness. Out of the blurry vision of his left eye, he saw Ras, Sahu and Khetnu approaching from across the tracks.

"Life's a tube filled with hot air until it goes phussss!" he mused to himself, watching the persistence of his pursuers. He limped off into the woods to create distance between him and his pursuers. He hurried along the foot trail through lush forest overlooking Tantalus Harbor and sweeping down from the nearly 60-km-long crest line of mountains that are the main watershed area. He glanced at a couple of small feral chickens – a gaudy cock strutting around his brownish hen. He fumbled with Sweet Dreams still tucked in his waist but the birds obviously didn't want his company and ran off into the dense undergrowth. The trail was narrow and the lush forest was unfamiliar.

He glanced over his shoulder and saw Ras and Sahu closing ground on him. He had entered a cluster of small white flowers with yellow centers, and large leaves that look a bit like sycamore. Neru smelled the pine trees growing wild, and rested for a moment. The lovely, flutelike warbling of the white-rumped shama, mingled with the more familiar song of the Japanese bush warbler. The mixture was bewildering. Neru felt tired. He hid behind a huge tree that appeared to be hundreds of years old. He felt he could not go on anymore and chose to die here under the sycamore tree. As Sahu approached, Neru heard the huge branch suddenly dropping and looked up in time to receive the hit on the head.

Chapter 22: Divine Taskmaster

Customers who patronize New York's Tatunen restaurant for dinner were mostly clean-cut, wealthy, and they enjoyed the open-air bar. Tatunen is located in an area that is considered a red-light district, full of streetwalkers and unregulated astrology and massage clubs. In the last few years, it has also become a hub for spiritual readings, a teenage-hangout district, even an old-ladies-walking-their-dogs district. It's a pretty interesting place to spend an evening: it's an anything-goes nuthouse.

Across the street is Geb Hetep, a multilevel yoga club in an old mansion. It has housed everything from a health clinic to meditation and Reiki units and now features a yoga studio plus themed mini-lounges.

But Tet-Sebau is the heart of local night life. It is a disco housed in an old butcher shop decorated with meat hooks and neon signs and after-hours parties that go well past daybreak, ironically with many vegetarian options on the menu. In the basement of Tet-Sebau is a sign less, cavelike, labyrinth nightclub. Nobody seems to know its real name.

It was here that Ra Heru Khuti tracked down Sethe. He was bent on killing Sethe for sadistically attempting to murder his mother Amseth and for what Ap did to Bast. Sekhet had killed Ap, an imposter of Apep who was still alive. Both Ap and Apep had many forms. But before Ra Heru Khuti could get Sethe, he knew he had to get his henchman, Apep, first.

Ra Heru Khuti entered the Tet-Sebau Club where one of Apep's animals, the infamous Popobawa, had recently struck causing panic in the Tet-Sebau Club clients. The "creature," described as a dwarf with bat-like wings and ears, and sharp talons, is feared for its nasty habit of sucking its victim's blood while they sleep. The result is a paralysis of sorts where the victims experience either a sense of being weighted down and unable to move, or floating sensations as if the essence of their being is separated from their bodies. All of Popobawa's recent victims have been linked to the Tet-Sebau Club. The animal can be detected by an acrid smell or the sight of a cloud of smoke. Sometimes, it is visible to everyone except the terrified victim. It is believed to take human form by day, but with pointed fingers. After doing its vile deed, the Popobawa instructs its frightened victims to spread the word about their ordeal or helplessly await its return to feed once again on their flesh and blood. Local hospitals have treated numerous broken ribs, bruises, wounds, lacerations and other injuries attributed to the animal.

Seated in the far side of the Tet-Sebau Club, Ra Heru Khuti pretended to drink a draft beer. He was about to give up on his search when the acrid smell hit his nose. He knew his search paid off when he also saw smoke coming from the far corner of the bar. Smoking was prohibited in the club. Instantly, he drew the bottle of specially prepared Dark Deceased bath Sekhet had given him to ward off Apep. He poured some of the bath in his hand and threw it in the direction of the corner where the smoke was and immediately it blazed into a ball of fire.

"What the heck! That hurts!" The invisible voice screamed as it fled through the back door. Ra Heru Khuti gave chase out back, over the fence, across the street and through the cemetery. He tracked Popobawa just past the ball field near Emily's Bridge, a known hide out for the Sebau.

Many refused to cross Emily's bridge after dark. It is said that a dark deceased named Emily haunts the bridge, and she's not just a spooky specter that allows the watcher a fleeting glimpse before vanishing back into nothingness. This dark deceased is feared as she is known for shaking cars and slashing victims with iron claws. Numerous cars have been mysteriously clawed. People have heard a woman's voice and witnessed strange lights at Emily's Bridge. Photographs taken here, often develop improperly without explanation, and many have found whispy streaks appearing in the photos. Legend has it that Emily was a jilted lover who hung herself from the bridge three hundred years ago.

Ra Heru Khuti reached into his pocket, extracted some white powder and scattered it in the air. As the powder settled, a number of footprints appeared on the bridge. Then numerous forms took shape. In the dark, Ra Heru Khuti stood in the center of the bridge and listened attentively. While no distinctly human voices were heard, more footsteps became audible, accompanied by loud grunting. At the end of the bridge a very loud, babbling brook howled through the wooded surroundings. Only the brave dared to enter the bridge after dark.

Beyond Emily's bridge near the ball field was what seemed like a neglected patch of land. It was a tiny triangle located outside the old mill, south of the Temple Mount. Here, underneath the stones, weeds, and rubble was Jeremiah's Pit. This is where Jeremiah was hung. Named after the sixteenth century BCE prophet, Jeremiah predicted that the slave trade would end and America would be lost and her people exiled throughout the world. Jeremiah was a free Black man, and when the local townspeople couldn't stand hearing so much doom and gloom, they lured him into the area, captured and hanged him.

Ra Heru Khuti climbed to the roof of the Mount, looked down and thought he saw something moving by the spring, also known as the Shiloh. The only natural water source in the entire area, the bountiful local Gihon originates in rain that falls on the Mount and seeps through the region's porous limestone. Although the water appears to flow continuously, it actually gushes out at regular intervals several times a day. Ra Heru Khuti jumped down to get a better view of the area. He followed the path down the steps, to the left, and into a tunnel. The steep descent stopped at the edge of a vertical shaft. He looked up, standing at the edge of the shaft, to see a distinct crack in the wall and noticed that the rock above the crack was of a different appearance from the rock below. He peered through the crack and saw a gigantic pool, which channeled water from the spring.

Moving with the speed of light, he tracked down the Popobawa who sprang out of the pool and burst recklessly through the crack in the wall, falling onto the tracks of the oncoming Ameritrak train. Ra Heru Khuti knelt down beside the Popobawa who screamed from the pain of Ra Heru Khuti's strike he felt in his chest. He held both of the Popobawa's arms locked under his armpits and smashed his head into his chest as the bright lights of the train grew bigger and nearer. The animal fought back but its struggle was futile. As the train switched tracks, the beast's leg was trapped between the switching tracks. He couldn't move.

When the Popobawa realized it could not escape the grip of Ra Heru Khuti whose strength had grown immensely, he changed form and revealed his true nature. He struggled but it was no use.

Ra Heru Khuti stepped back off the tracks and smiled at the frantic beast.

"Sethe!" Ra Heru Khuti called out fettering him. "Your day of reckoning has finally come!" Ra Heru Khuti was surprised, for Sethe had many illusions. He grabbed both of Sethe's hands and stretched him out over the tracks. He would make sure the train ran over his body.

But as the train approached, a bright blue light descended in the mist and out of it emerged the Divine Taskmaster-Tehuti, standing tall with his outstretched hand. Ra Heru Khuti recognized the Ibis ring with a blue gem on Tehuti's finger and the Uas scepter he carried in his hand. He glanced over at Ra Heru Khuti and commanded, "Let him go!"

"Why should I let him go?" Ra Heru Khuti protested to the Holy One.

"Why should you kill him?" Tehuti-the Divine Taskmaster queried raising the blue parchment he held in his hand. "Can you declare in your heart you are above sin?" Tehuti again queried.

"He has caused much harm in the world." Ra Heru Khuti declared. "He caused wars, killing millions and leaving millions ravaged. He created chaos and misery, and brought grief and dread to countless others! He invented new financial crimes, stealing from millions, rendering many bankrupt; and those he could not steal from he made homeless. Look around!" Ra Heru Khuti declared.

"You know the eleven laws. Because you are the son of Ra, you are the Ausar and, therefore, accountable for all of your actions. It's not for you to judge but if you are without sin, proceed!" Tehuti replied sternly.

"He created the greed that has driven people to envy, wrath, and jealousy!" Ra Heru Khuti laid accusation against the Lawless One.

"They wanted it. Why blame me for this mess?" Sethe argued. By now, Sethe's confederacy had arrived and taken up position beside him near the track. They flanked Ra Heru Khuti.

"Bankers are getting massive bonuses and the politicians are lining their own pockets while people starve." Ra Heru Khuti continued to point out to Tehuti.

"Where are your readings?" Tehuti asked.

"He caused harm to my mother Amseth," he again implored Tehuti.

"Let him go!" Tehuti told him sending a burst of sky blue and white lightning against the tracks that released Sethe's feet. Sethe, seeing there was a stalemate between Tehuti and Ra Heru Khuti, took advantage and disappeared into the night with his henchmen.

"How can you cause such a madman to go free when he has broken all of the laws of Maat?" Ra Heru Khuti asked Tehuti.

"Even Sethe has his place in the world!" Tehuti told him as he disappeared into the night.

Ra Heru Khuti boarded the train. The train thundered through the hills somewhere in Pennsylvania. Ra Heru Khuti watched intensely as the Amish men on board the train broke out a deck of *Metu Neter* cards and consulted the Oracles. The café car attendant, using an iPod and a set of portable speakers, broadcast Miles Davis "Round Midnight" on his speakers.

"Life gets discombobulating," the attendant remarked amidst the stillness of the night.

Ra Heru Khuti glanced through the windows on the train. American night scenery unfolded. A dirty layer of ice and snow subdued the still cropland in the distant horizon. At a nearby table a woman was buried up to her nose in a novel and a college kid pecked at a laptop. Overlaying all of this was the soundtrack: choo-k-choo- k-choo-k-choo-k-choo-k – the metronomic rhythm of an Ameritrak train rolling to its destination.

Chapter 23: Sethian Confederacy

It turns out that the men who were driving in the black Mercedes and who grabbed Sabu in front of the Het Neter brought him to the local precinct for questioning. They were Sethian agents assigned to infiltrate local drug scenes. For two weeks they kept Sabu imprisoned, demanding the whereabouts of the *Papyrus Am Tuat*. Each time Sabu said he didn't know, they brutally beat him. It was clear that even though they were cops they worked for Sethe. After two weeks of torture, they released him only to surround his home with a huge task force a week later and take him back to prison.

After two months of imprisonment he was allowed to write to his family since they were not given permission to visit. Sabu sat down to write a letter to his sons from behind the prison bars. He entitled the letter, *"Where Daddy At?"* He began the letter by asking "How is Mommy doing? And went on to explain that he was an activist for peace and those who chose the course of change had to be prepared to sacrifice. Part of his sacrifice, he told his boys, was that he had not been able to spend as much time with them as he would have liked. He finished by writing that life is always tenuous, and that at some point Sethe's agents can take you away. He hoped they would come to understand his mission and "take up the legacy of struggle."

Sabu remembered the second arrest. Early that morning Sethian agents came with a force that was beyond Sabu's wildest imaginings. They cordoned off the block, took up positions on the rooftops, and waited for their target to walk the last hundred yards to his Brooklyn home. Before Sabu noticed the unnatural quiet that had settled on his neighborhood, he found himself surrounded by about thirty of Sethe's armed agents serving on the city's Joint Terrorist Taskforce.

"It was as if they came up out of the ground," Sabu later recalled. Once the agents had him inside a patrol car they used bullhorns to announce the names of people they knew to be in Sabu's house warning them to surrender. Within minutes, Kaheri and Satra Maat walked out onto the sidewalk into the glare of floodlights and rifle barrels. All this firepower to arrest one individual who the Taskforce believed had the *Papyrus Am Tuat* or knew its whereabouts?

Ra Heru Khuti and his associates had been under surveillance for almost a year. Moments before Sabu's house was seized, an even larger team of agents had arrested another man named Ifa Dare they believed may have had the *Papyrus Am Tuat*. In all, about four hundred agents of the Taskforce stormed and searched six homes, one in New Jersey, one in Westchester County and the rest scattered across the five boroughs of New York City. When the operation was over, only Ifa Dare and Sabu were jailed under the new federal Bail Reform Act, which, for a time, allowed the government to hold inmates in so-called preventive detention, without bail and without charge.

Sethe's Taskforce was enormous and it marked the end of one of the more exhaustive investigations – a network that used up to one hundred agents a day and relied on an intricate web of surveillance devices. In addition to a variety of fraud and weapons counts, the government charged the suspects with stealing a confidential national document-the *Papyrus Am Tuat*, refusing to reveal its whereabouts, resisting arrest and conspiring to facilitate the prison escapes of two incarcerated members of their organization. The conspiracy charges were brought under the racketeering statute, a law that's more commonly used against defendants involved in organized crime.

Months later, the spouses and a few friends of Sabu and Ifa Dare were also taken into custody and jailed for refusing to testify before various grand juries convened to investigate the case. The suspects all plead not guilty, and argued that everything about the case was motivated by a desire to control the *Papyrus Am Tuat*.

Two federal judges ruled against the use of preventive detention for the suspects, one of them stating, "The government failed to show a 'strong probability' or clear and convincing evidence of dangerousness."

The irony was bitter for Ifa Dare and Sabu. They were eventually released, but their spouses and friends remained behind bars. Ifa Dare spoke to defense lawyers for Kaheri and the others declaring "The struggle against Sethe and the Taskforce was nothing new. We are not just articulate. We are intelligent and activists. We desire to re-write history. We are Sethe's worst fears. We do community outreach, educating the public about the legitimacy of armed struggle and self defense. We are young, strapped and don't give a damn!" Ifa Dare boasted.

The defense lawyers for Kaheri, Satra Maat and the other defendants argued that government action against them was a nightmare and psychologically traumatic because state sanctioned violence by the Sethian Taskforce led to their arrests. Angry talk and provocative ideas, the lawyers pointed out, are protected in the First Amendment to the U. S. Constitution. In an amicus brief filed on behalf of the defendants by a group of pro-bono lawyers and city council members, they wrote: "The most that the evidence shows is that the defendants allegedly may disagree with the present system of government surveillance, threats of violence and unsubstantiated detention. Furthermore, the allegations that the defendants may have acquired or trained themselves in the use of weapons, is no crime. Let the court note that said defendants also advocate a peaceful solution to their problems. To make such beliefs and conduct the basis for a criminal prosecution is not only illegal it is not justifiable."

The Sethian Taskforce and agents saw the case differently. They shadowed the suspects round the clock for nine months, collecting volumes of notes and taping up to five hundred conversations. In that time, no major criminal acts were witnessed. Yet, according to the agents, the suspects seemed to be carefully plotting, even rehearsing, violent holdups and jailbreaks. Worried about possible killings, the authorities finally moved in before anything specific happened. The raids appeared to support the government's concerns. An arsenal of weapons, including Uzi semi automatic rifles and sawed-off shotguns, were found at several of the houses searched.

Chapter 24: Freedom Fighters

Ra Heru Khuti found himself seated at a round table on the eleventh floor of the Metropolitan Correction Center, the federal jail adjacent to the offices of the US attorneys who oversaw the Taskforce that had been following his every step for the last year. The uniform he wore, a jumpsuit colored orange to denote maximum security, was peeled down to the waistband, revealing long-sleeved, long underwear. A slightly scraggy beard framed his long face, met his sideburns, and disappeared under a black crocheted skullcap. He arranged various documents in neat piles – one pile had his "Personal Statement to Family, Friends and Community Supporters," a second pile consisted of sheets of yellow lined paper with handwritten notes outlining the specific points he wanted to cover in the interview.

Ra Heru Khuti's lawyer, sat besides him to his right. He was also an Associate Professor of Criminal Justice at Rutgers University and the former National Director of the National Conference of Black Lawyers.

One of the major topics on Ra Heru Khuti's agenda was the "heinous" behavior of the Sethian government. To explain it, Ra

Heru Khuti had constructed a "four tiered paradigm," something he said, "had to do with developing a Sethian model with certain theories that could be put into operation. The paradigm was extremely intricate, having not only four tiers but within the tiers numbered sections and subsections. That's how complicated Sethe's network is." He told them.

At times, Ra Heru Khuti's loquaciousness threatened to overwhelm his lucidity, but there was no missing the message. The government's purpose, he said, was to, "surgically remove key opposition from off the streets, and to thwart their ability to organize people."

None of the defendants would deny for a second that they had walked right up to the line separating constitutionally protected behavior from criminality. But their lawyers argued in court, that in terms of the more serious charges, the line was never crossed. Ra Heru Khuti's lawyer declared in a memo on the fixing of bail, "This is a conspiracy case, but these people are not accused of talking together about the best way to sell narcotics. Rather, these defendants spoke with each other, about the varying and numerous alternatives available to those who are dedicated to the concept of social and racial equality."

As Ra Heru Khuti talked, he centered himself in the front of the room. He explained that the central contradiction for all revolutionaries was that talk would never get the job done.

"Fundamentally," Ra Heru Khuti said, "there has to be a revolution!" The vehemence of this last declaration made him sober.

Ifa Dare seized the moment when he said "We are in an antithetical and confrontational relationship with Sethian forces, not because we are exposing their contradictions to the public but because our advocacy for truth, our militancy for righteousness, peace and equality makes us freedom fighters."

Ra Heru Khuti stood up and said "The only reason I am shackled is because of the *Papyrus Am Tuat*! The bottom line is the *Papyrus Am Tuat* will not fall into Sethe's hands." He announced looking into the double sided mirror on the wall. He knew Sethe and his henchmen stood on the other side listening to their conversation. "But then again, I didn't say that, did I?" he finished with a smile.

Chapter 25: Make Money and Keep Pushin'

Ras had never given his dreams much thought, and by his mid forties he had drawn a tight line around his existence. Inside it he found a form of contentment that flowed from the absence of hunger or risk. He was not where he was supposed to be. He was working with Sahu for Sethe and he was dancing a half step ahead of the grim reaper. But he had a decent place to stay and a woman named Matilda who loved him enough to put up with his mood swings.

If his life was a flirtation with poverty then, at least he was one of the working poor. Except at love, in fact, he counted himself lucky. He was never out of work, not even when he was adrift between steady jobs for a year. He did day labor for the minimum wage and hustled other gigs on the side. He considered any job better than welfare and two jobs better than one; no matter what kind of job or what kind of money. He worked days in a paint factory and moonlighted as a janitor in his apartment complex when he met Sahu. The wage at the plant was as good as he had ever made, nearly ten dollars an hour, and his basement flat was rent free. If he had managed his finances better, he

156

thought, he could have been living "pretty medium," the only phrase he could find for his minimalist hope. He seemed to have a hard time making lasting connections; he had about him the air of a man constantly reckoning the odds on the profitability of human relationships.

Twenty years after the collapse of his first marriage, he was still haunted by the feeling that he had blown it all emotionally and relationships had become as impermanent as his jobs and his bank account. He had power over women, for he played on their insecurities, made promises that lay deep inside his hazel eyes, and exploited such vulnerable women. He fathered a daughter by one woman and a son by another, five months apart, and moved on. The mothers got to be friends so his children could grow up knowing each other. The women also bonded because the unreliability of men was something they had in common.

Ras did try marriage another time, eleven years after the first one ended. He was working part time as an attendant in a laundromat, trying to pay the bills during the winter layoff season in the construction trade. She was a customer, a lady named Barbara with two children of her own. He was attentive. She responded. She began bringing in her laundry three times a week and lunch for Ras. He shut down early one day and met her at the seaport. They started seeing other. He was broke. She was sympathetic.

"You paying that high rent," she said, "Come live with me!" He did, and for a time he didn't need money. But when they married after three or four years together, she changed her ways and wanted him to change his. He was suddenly the man of the house, the breadwinner. She was piling on the burdens, more than he could handle. He had been fired from one job. Another job folded under him. The mother of one of his children had pressed the family court for child support. He couldn't produce what Barbara was demanding, and she wouldn't back off. She picked fights, became loud with him, broke things around the house and then called the police on him.

The time came when Ras could no longer live with her nagging and his own failure as provider. He chose to move on. But they still saw each other for they were still emotionally bonded. She claimed he would always be the man for her and have a special place in her heart. She went back to her church and called him often to talk about the men that were interested in her.

"The women are saying that there is something wrong with me because I don't respond to the men who express interest in me," Barbara told Ras. "But I can't see another person until I am over you. You and I are one. You complement me. I long for you when you are not around. I miss cuddling up to you and feeling your body heat. I could never meet another man who is as gentle and attentive as you." She lied to him.

Ras would drop in on Barbara, unannounced, to pick up his painting gear for his job and one day he found her with another man. He paid them no attention and went about his business and finished painting. He said he had to "make the money and keep on pushin'."

He might have been summing up his life. He had spent it at a succession of unskilled and semiskilled jobs, most of them vulnerable and none very rewarding except for the money. He thought of them mostly as elbow-and-ass work. He had a mind too, and he wished he could use it. But the boss didn't pay him for his mind, he told himself. Folks never think you got any sense, and they hated for you to show them you do. You would see them do something wrong around the plant, try to put a part backwards or some foolishness, and you couldn't say anything – you just had to sit there and wait until they figured it out. So Ras eased silently on through his days, doing what he got paid for and smiling all the time. They thought he was dumb, he guessed, but they were going to think that any damn way. He knew what time it was.

It was true Ras thought Sethian folks ran things and didn't cut him any breaks. But he wasn't the kind to blame them alone for the way his life had dead-ended. He saw his own part in it; he regretted that he hadn't stayed in school and that he had thrown away his money on the pleasures of the moment instead of buying a little piece of real estate or something. At the margin of life, where he lived, you couldn't tell whether the man wasn't hiring you because of what you looked like or because he just didn't need help. So he lived inside his self imposed limits, seeing no way out and no higher destiny to pursue even if he could. His wages were garnished last winter to satisfy a bad note he had co-signed, and he had to sell his jewelry and TV to get his car repaired. For a time the plant shut down, and except for his janitor job he had no work at all.

His two children were in their teens. He provided what he could for them, but he was an absentee daddy to his son in town and his first and favorite, Sherri, now seventeen, was in St. Louis somewhere with her mother or grandmother – he had lost track.

What had changed in his life was the tempo. He felt nearer than ever to repose. The anchor of his life was his new wife, Matilda, a quiet lady with a lot of gold on her fingers and pleasant smiles. It was like she colored gold. Ras thought she was cute. She was nice, too, a lady with a job of her own, no kids and no obvious desire except to please him. He had recently given her a one hundred dollar bill, and she hadn't even busted it yet. She was saving it to buy him a watch for his birthday. The day they met was like a smile from Lady Luck, the first Ras had known since his teenage marriage broke up. Ras was seeing someone else then, and so was Matilda; her old man in those days was a guy that Ras drank beer with. But one night Ras and his woman got into a fight that ended with her throwing his things out the window. Matilda's old man happened to walk by in the midst of the storm and helped him pick up afterward.

"If you don't have nowhere to go," he told him, "you can spend the night on the couch." The overnight guest became a boarder, at forty dollars a week. The arrangement suited Matilda's old man at first. He was out of work and needed money. But he kept disappearing into his drugs, and Matilda kicked him out, inviting Ras to stay in his place. When Ras and Matilda found their new place, her old man helped them move.

Ras was still there in the waning days of winter, the underground man, living in his basement apartment out of sight of the larger world. There was too much happening out there, he thought, and nothing, that is except work. He almost never went downtown. He preferred the safety of his place – Ras in the half light with a cold beer and a warm smoke and the glow of the TV playing over the bare wood floor. There remained trace elements of regret in his life, but he wasn't crying. He had made his choices and was making the best of them.

While he couldn't honestly say he was happy, he thought he would be, if he found the *Papyrus Am Tuat* for his boss, Sethe. He expected to be rewarded.

Chapter 26: Child Soldiers

Khetnu knew Sahu had found Neru. He tried not to guess the outcome as he sat outside on a bench rolling a joint. He knew he had failed his friend. He felt as if everything was caving in on him and he had to find a way out of nowhere. He was arrested twice today in his effort to roll a joint. The first time he was arrested he was thinking about how tired he was and never saw the plain clothes officers approaching him until they had handcuffed him for rolling a marijuana cigarette. Released after posting one hundred dollars bond, Khetnu returned about an hour later to a different bench on the same street, where police again found him rolling a joint.

He was tired of the life he lived. He was a disappointment to his mother and sister, Meri Ab. She needed him to be there for her. She was growing up fast and he had to be there to keep knuckle heads away from her. Most of all, he wanted a way out from Sahu, Ras and the street life.

Khetnu recently shaved his head as a symbol of the change he needed to make in his life. He was uncertain about a lot of things. He was silent for a while watching his neighbors who live in fear of young men like him hanging out at the street corner selling drugs. He was thankful to the family that adopted him and his sister and brought them to America. He tried to live up to their expectations until a few years ago when he met Neru. Since then he had become rebellious and disrespectful, a reminder of his childhood.

Silently, Khetnu tried to erase earlier memories of his childhood in Rwanda. Now, sitting outside on a bench with a cigarette in his hand, the memories began to flood his head. America did not shield him from the things he did as a child to stay alive.

Khetnu remembered the shaved head and gun slung across his back as he stood guard alone at the perimeter of the camp. He was uncertain about a lot of things, even his young age. A quiet voice said he might have been eleven years old because he was a baby when his mother wrapped him with the last of her possessions and made her escape across the border. Asked where he was from, he gestured toward the lush hills rippling to the east. Somewhere among them was an unmarked land frontier and a country he called Rwanda. Khetnu didn't know if his parents were alive or dead. He didn't remember much except his mother carried him across the border, out of Rwanda. But then something happened to her. He was left alone and the other people in the refugee camp looked after him. His father was a soldier. He just disappeared.

Khetnu fell silent again for a while, watching his neighbors eye him suspiciously as they walked past him. His memories never left him. He only pretended they were not there. He never spoke to his adopted parents of his life as a child in the Congo. "It was the Tutsis who are to blame for this predicament," he said to himself. He hated them all. "They stole my country, Rwanda - a Hutu country," he reasoned.

There was something in Khetnu's voice when he says the word "Tutsis." It was the power of the word to conjure up the horror of the murder of hundreds of thousands in the Rwandan genocide. When the Tutsi rebels took over the Rwanda's government, the Hutu exodus began and the boy's life changed irrevocably. He became one of the child soldiers. Sometimes he was responsible for appalling atrocities. Other times it was because his mind had been twisted by the powerful drugs he was given to sedate him from the hellish life he was forced to live. After years of invasion, civil war and slaughter, he became engrossed in genocide. He was part of a second generation of killers reared on hate and imbued with the ideology of extermination of the Tutsis. Some of the other child soldiers learned it from fathers who were responsible for the mass killings initially, back in Rwanda. Others, like Khetnu, were raised by the extremist Hutu rebels.

Khetnu remembered sitting alone, guarding the perimeter of the camp that was deep in the mountains, south of the Congolese city of Bukavu. The camp was little more than a dozen or so mud brick and wood huts with grass roofs. Inside the camp he saw a handful of soldiers sitting around. Some wore the same uniforms as government troops – plain olive green, with black boots. Others wore brightly colored T-shirts. They carried larger-caliber weapons with belts of bullets slung across their shoulders. There was a rusting rim of an old car wheel dangling from a nearby tree as an alarm. He was supposed to beat it as hard as he could if the enemy approached. He was the youngest fighter there – most of the others were in their late teens. They boasted about three thousand fighters, hundreds of them children or youths, and they were the largest of the militias in eastern Congo. He was one of many boys recruited at ten years old to fight. At that he was worse than the older ones because they didn't know Rwanda, they didn't know any Tutsis. They just hated them as the enemy. All they knew was "The Tutsis stole our country and they killed the Hutus or made them slaves. We had to kill them wherever they were. It was the only way to get our country back. When they are defeated I can go home," he would repeat to himself. Up in the hills he learned a terrible lesson: that a gun could get him what he wanted – food and money.

When Khetnu made it back to Rwanda, he discovered that it was not easy to return to what passed for a normal life especially since the only school he had ever known was the army. Being reunited with his sister in foster home was a miracle. The chiefs were looking for boys who thought of going back to Rwanda. If they found him they would certainly kill him as an example. He had a friend who was hanged from a tree because he had the idea to go back to Rwanda. In the foster home which was a colonial-era house in the hills around Masisi in North Kivu, Khetnu welcomed the news that he and his sister were adopted by an American family.

As Khetnu sat outside on the bench smoking a cigarette he wanted to be free of past memories that clouded his mind. America did not shield him from the unforgivable acts he had committed as a child to stay alive.

He opened his eyes and noticed the beautiful flow of men and women dressed in red and white niong ting. He had no idea what he was doing but he got off the bench, put the cigarette out and followed the flow of red and white niong ting into the huge courtyard. He took a seat in the back, noticed the faces looking at him strangely, but paid them no attention.

His sprit led him here for a reason. He tapped his feet as the *Djembe* drumming got more intense. Khetnu could no longer resist the impelling rhythms. His feet started tapping the floor involuntarily. As he breathed in he could see his body swelling up, turning red hot; ruby red, fiery red, transparent and getting hotter and hotter by the second. He could feel the fire burning up all the impurities within him, burning up all the foolish thoughts, burning up the coward within him. It burned up all the fears inside of him. Yes, he was as red-hot as fire.

Devoid of training in Kamitic cosmology, he could not control his thoughts; even though his spirit claimed this energy. It was as if he was out of his body but looking at himself expanding way up into the sky, growing taller and taller. Then he saw his head become the head of a hawk. He felt faint as he floated then he soared above everything. He was flying above all his conditionings, all obstructions and obstacles. He had the power. He flew as a huge gigantic hawk above everything, traveling through the stratosphere. He looked down on the tiny planet, Earth below him before his descent. Slowly with each breath he descended landing on the ground. But it didn't stop there. He shrank in size until he was like an ant, a little red ant, tiny and yet glowing under the sun.

Then Khetnu was lying flat on his back on the hot desert sand, glowing all over and feeling red hot like red amber. He heard a voice saying over and over again. "You are Heru ruler over the kingdom on Earth! Peace through adversity. What did Nelson

Mandela say? What did Ya Asantewaa say? What did Am Mesh
Nefertari say? What did Malcolm X say? You can take the King
or the Queen Mother away but you will never be able to take the
Golden Stool!" He was calm, free and at peace, smoldering over
an internal fire of memories. Yes, he was fire! His freedom was
his savior. His freedom restored mastery over his spirit; freedom
from domination, freedom from pleasure, freedom from pain,
freedom from sensualism, freedom to know and understand who
he is such that not even illness could harm him. He had gone to
that place of no-thing-ness and understood that from that point
forward he had the freedom to choose to do what was right. The
voice inside kept saying, "Pledge! Pledge to put at least one
negative behavior behind you once and for all. Pledge to put at
lease one pleasure, one dislike, and one emotion behind you
now!"

He was on the ritual floor turning around and around like a
spinning top without getting dizzy, without feeling nauseous.
"Heru is your freedom to say, 'No' to every single conditioning,
to every single desire and passion. You have no excuse! Heru
comes to end all excuses!" Still deep in trance, he felt someone's
hands spinning him around and around and around. Soon he was
exhausted and collapsed to the floor. He could feel the person
kneel beside him, whispering in his ear. He could feel her warm,
soft breasts against his chest. And he wept. The tears of relief

poured out of his eyes as the smooth fire caressed his heart. He wept for Neru and for his brothers and sisters who never made it out of the Congo, out of the Barrios, out of the Slums and out of the Ghettos. He wept and wept.

Chapter 27: Men Nefer and Anu

Ur Aua Un Nefer Hetep, as the head of the twin-cities of Men Nefer and Anu, in the Southern Country knew that much of his job revolved around a simple equation: the number of girls who get married is roughly equal to the number of new homes his community will need to accommodate its rapid growth. Last year Ur Aua Un Nefer Hetep oversaw the construction of two hundred houses and apartments, mostly on the outer-lying lots along the eastern edge of this four square mile community, a Kamitic enclave about sixty miles north of midtown Manhattan. By the end of the year, he said, Men Nefer will most likely have more than three hundred new homes.

"There are three tenets that drive the growth of our community: first, couples marry young, second they don't use birth control, and third, after couples get married they stay in the twin-cities of Men Nefer and Anu to build their family." Ur Aua Un Nefer Hetep continued, "Our growth comes simply from the fact that those who chose to have families have a lot of children." He added, "…and we need to build homes to respond to the needs of our community."

Land is a finite resource to the growing community. As the boundaries of Men Nefer and Anu extended beyond their borders, nearby neighbors in the towns of Buxton and Pinegrove are moving aggressively to prevent the community from expanding.

Men Nefer's population leaped to 11, 300 last year from 9,100 in 2009 and 7,400 in 2008 making it one of the fastest growing places in the state, according to the most recent estimates by the Census Bureau. For two years, developers and local officials of Men Nefer and its twin city, Anu, have been searching for private parcels in surrounding communities, hoping to expand through annexation for the third time since it was incorporated in 1987. After its incorporation, most of the growth was driven by migration from New York City for a better quality of life. But now, new arrivals are mostly babies and grooms coming to marry one of the local women.

Many families in Men Nefer fled the crowded streets of the five boroughs of New York City, for the cleaner air, safer communities and the open spaces of the twin cities, where the closest neighbor may not be so close by.

"We are hard-working people who decided to move here to pay fewer taxes and enjoy the quiet country," said Ur Aua Un Nefer Hetep, a retired New York City Transit Officer and leader of this community. "It's a shame that we had to form a city for no other reason but to preserve this peaceful and communal way of life," said Ur Aua Un Nefer Hetep. He continued, "Over the years there have been disputes over water pipelines and whether the local schools should receive state funding and benefits."

The community members felt a deep connection to the land. They were led here by Ur Aua Un Nefer Hetep, who saw it as an ideal place to raise large families away from the influences of the outside world.

The cities of Men Nefer and Anu each have two parks and several playgrounds. A network of sidewalks cross the cities so community members are able to walk to the acupuncture and Qi Gong clinics or organic supermarkets. Baby strollers are everywhere; in the lobbies of buildings or sidewalks and outside the stores.

"This is a great place to raise our children; it's easy to keep them away from distractions of the city," boasted Ur Aua Un Nefer Hetep. The median age in the city is twenty compared to thirty-five for the nation.

Ur Aua Un Nefer Hetep lived on a dead end street in a private home. On the other side of his home beside the lake are the radio and television center, adjacent to the Department of Communications. Ur Aua Un Nefer Hetep owns several of the business in the city. His wives help him run the businesses. Most women in Men Nefer are married soon after graduation from college, and they work until they give birth. Those who become stay-at-home mothers and wives assist the mothers who choose to return to work with childcare and household duties. The men, meanwhile, are mostly self-employed. Every man in the city has a skill or profession. Because of the sheer size of the families (the average household here has six people, but it is not uncommon for couples to have eight or ten children), and because the vast majority of households subsist on only one salary, sixty percent of the local families live modestly. Some even rely on public assistance, which is another sore point with neighboring communities.

The twin-cities of Men Nefer and Anu celebrate marriage and children. New families are always welcome.

Chapter 28: Conspiracy

So it went, day in and day out. It's easy to imagine how the Sethians must have felt. What were they doing? If it was an adult version of hide and seek, then the Taskforce was wasting its time, not to mention a great deal of tax revenue. But here and there, the Sethian agents saw something that convinced them they were on the right track in assuming that Ra Heru Khuti was trying to auction off the *Papyrus Am Tuat* to the highest bidder.

Sethe was given details on Ra Heru Khuti's modus operandi and his activities in keeping the *Papyrus Am Tuat* concealed until he sold it. The strategies included safe house, evasive maneuvers, and codes. The informants gave detailed testimony about escape routes Ra Heru Khuti used and also how he planned to sell the papyrus. Sethe's agents claim that on January twenty-seventh, just a month after they started intensive surveillance, they saw Ra Heru Khuti sitting in his car taking notes in front of St. John's the Divine Church. After an hour or so Ra Heru Khuti allegedly followed a priest to the B'nai Brith building. A few hours later, he checked in at yet a third building; the Free Mason building on Twenty-Third Street and Seventh Avenue in Manhattan.

Ra Heru Khuti arrived at this location before the Rabbi that followed him from the B'nai Brith building and then lingered about window shopping until the arrival of the *Papyrus Am Tuat*," the agent reported. Once the truck arrived, Ra Heru Khuti moved to a corner pay phone from which he observed the unloading of the document, the agent claimed. That morning, Ra Heru Khuti also found time to drive to the Pan Am Heliport at East Sixtieth Street and the East River and apparently asked about flight rates and schedules. Later, he drove to a second heliport, at Thirty-Fourth Street.

Still, later that day Ra Heru Khuti and Satra Maat were seen at the Brooklyn House of Detention, where they were visiting Sabu. Sethe's agents claimed that Ra Heru Khuti was observed calling Satra Maat attention to the top of the jail. Six days later, Ifa Dare was seen at the Thirty-Fourth Street heliport allegedly asking questions about whether a helicopter could be used in a rescue operation without tipping over, how much fuel it carried, what communication it maintained with the ground, and which buttons in the cockpit did what. A few days later he was allegedly observed at the Brooklyn House of Detention, "apparently pacing off distances and counting windows on the jail." The agents began to believe that they were planning to free Sabu by landing a helicopter on the roof of the Brooklyn House of Detention.

Around this time, the New York Police reported an odd occurrence. They received a tip of a possible robbery at an Art Gallery in Brooklyn; the NYPD installed a stakeout. Shortly after the armored truck pulled into the terminal, two uniformed policemen drove into the area, unaware of the stakeout or the tip. Suddenly, all hell broke loose. A parked Buick with Sethe's agents blinked its lights; a Rabbi at one corner of the nearby intersection started to wave his hands franticly, yelled and ran towards a Mustang parked near the art gallery. A black van and the Mustang raced off into the night. The police caught up with one man who was carrying a bulging briefcase. Its contents included a fully loaded nine millimeter handgun with a defaced serial number.

Chapter 29: Waiting for the Revolution

The activities of the suspects declined over the summer months –
perhaps, as the Taskforce believes, because of an aborted action.
But the tempo of the investigation picked up at the end of
August, after the agents received permission to plant wiretaps
and microphones in the Ebbets Field apartments. Sethe believed
he was getting closer to regain the *Papyrus Am Tuat.* On
September fourth, agents listened in on a conversation that
sounded to them like a training session to break into a Museum,
steal the Rosetta Stone Papyrus and insert the *Papyrus Am Tuat.*
Accompanied by the sound of frequent dry-firing of weapons, a
man who Sethe's agents believe is Ra Heru Khuti was heard
instructing another male, "It is easy for me to sit here and tell
those who have transgressed against me that it's alright. The only
punishment I see for you is that you must cut off the heads of
Sethe and Apep. Return to the ways of the Shemsu Heru."

To the ears of government and Sethe's agents, these sounded
like careful preparations for murder. Yet there seemed to be a
problem among the suspects–who was going to do the killing?
Sabu, who was said to be skilled in the use of automatic

weapons, had recently suffered an injured leg. A week later, he had a more serious problem. At the time he was arrested, he had been on parole from an earlier gun possession conviction. He faced the possibility of either going to jail again or becoming a fugitive. Ra Heru Khuti himself apparently had been vacillating, arguing that Sabu should serve his time and return to his family. The group seemed to consider this opinion tantamount to treason. "True revolutionaries never go to jail if they can help it. They go underground!"

In a conversation overhead on September thirteenth, a woman believed to be Satra Maat referred to Ra Heru Khuti's vacillation as a "betrayal" in his absence.

A man believed to be Ifa Dare continued, "We love, we care but it cannot get in the way of our work. If you are ready to go with me to *Behutet*, to triumph over Sethe and Apep, if you are ready to cut off the heads of Sethe and Apep, there is no condition to what we do…I love you…but I will kill Sethe and Apep. If you betray us (sound of slide being racked on a semi-automatic pistol) without a second thought. That's my kind of love.

We have to put an end to all the lies, and fairy tales like Christopher Columbus discovered America. We risk our freedom to re-write history and to teach our children the truth. One day I hope to stand in a classroom and teach our children the truth about Christopher Columbus before he came to America. What did he do first? Where did he travel first? He went to Portugal and then he went down by the Niger River. He didn't sail from Portugal straight off to America. He went down to the River Niger. Now, if a man wants to go via west to India, why did he go down to the mouth of the Niger River? The Canary Islands? There was a tradition in Africa already where people traveled from the Canary Islands westward. The ocean surrounding the Canary Islands has what? The trade wind currents. So, at the Canary Islands, vessels ride a current that takes them straight to the Americas. You can't hit that trade wind from Portugal or from Spain. Now, how did he know to go to the mouth of the Niger River to the Canary Islands to catch the trade winds west....Come on now! And when you dig into it, you find that Christopher Columbus had a map because Africans had been sailing to the Americas long before him. There's a whole prehistoric tradition of the Indians trading with African people. That's what we find during the Olmec civilization. This is the history Van Sertima wrote about in his book *They Came Before Columbus*." Ifa Dare was very well read and spiritually cultivated so he always had a story to tell.

Shortly afterward, Ra Heru Khuti disappeared for several days, despite the efforts of the Sethian task force. When he reappeared, "carrying bags" of course, matters had turned from bad to worse.

The group had apparently planned an event of some kind – but because it had been scheduled to take place on a Jewish holiday, it had been canceled on the grounds that the streets would have been too crowded. A person believed to be Ra Heru Khuti said, "No guerilla in the world would accept the postponement." Later, the same speaker added, "The longer we keep …those elementary things that we are doing from happening…then the revolution never jumps off. And so you have people who are waiting in situations. Trapped, *Waiting For Godot*, waiting for the unconquerable peace, waiting for justice! Waiting for the revolution and it never comes. But they have it all wrong. There is truth in the slogan 'no peace, no justice.'"

There followed an intense discussion between the same speaker and a second male, allegedly Ifa Dare, about a "deadline," the "dress rehearsal," and the "jump." Finally, Ra Heru Khuti allegedly told Ifa Dare, "As of right now we are depending on you for three major things." Based on the conversations and other evidence, the Sethian Taskforce thought it knew what two of those major things were: an attempt to spring suspect Sabu from the Brooklyn Detention House and the possible robbery of Rosetta Stone Papyrus in Brooklyn. The suspects themselves seemed to sense that the circle around them was closing in.

Just two days later, a man telephoned Ra Heru Khuti and told him to look up the Gospel according to John, citing chapter and verse. The cited verse reads, "Then they sought to take him: but no man laid hands on him. Because his hour was not yet come." The following day agents following Ifa Dare saw him throw a box into a construction garbage dump. An agent retrieved the box, carefully put bits of torn paper together, and read the following note: "Dress rehearsal Wednesday should – should be Wednesday or Thursday evening." Comments followed about the cost of different guns. A separate piece of paper read, "find the cost and where available to buy-six foot nylon rope – nylon ladder which would hold one body weighing up to two hundred and fifty pounds."

Taskforce operatives now felt the real pressure. Despite all the work, the only crime was the alleged car robbery: what's more, they hadn't spotted any of the suspects with any known fugitives.

Chapter 30: Night of Final Battle

The U.S. Attorney's Office, which was monitoring the case on a day-by-day basis in the last two months decided to step in. "We had to make some judgments about letting this case go long enough so that there was evidence or what we regarded as evidence–clear evidence. But at the same time stepping in so that no one was severely harmed by it," said U.S. Attorney, Mike Blackburn.

The word went out to grab them. A team of three hundred of Sethe's Taskforce and agents was put together. A command post was set up at Twenty-Six Federal Plaza, and a plan was developed to capture the *Papyrus Am Tuat* first, then every one else. Latest reports indicated agents had been tracking Ra Heru Khuti through Times Square when he suddenly entered a building and disappeared. It was later confirmed through video surveillance by cameras around the building that he had climbed to the roof, crossed over to another building, and returned to the street from a door that was not being watched. For nearly three hours the task force combed the west side looking for him.

At two in the morning they found him at the Forty Second Street Pier waiting to board the boat that was receiving passengers destined for the city of Men Nefer. As he walked toward the gate, he saw Sethe and Apep pushing past the crowd to get to him. Behind him on the right, two black SUVs slammed on their brakes as agents hurried out of them with high power rifles over their shoulders.

Ra Heru Khuti put his head down and ran as fast as he could to the gate. He barely made it through when the gate closed. He ran up the planks and on the boat with a sense of relief. Ra Heru Khuti looked back and saw neither Sethe nor Apep. He concluded he had lost them. He made his way to the top deck and heard the engines turning over. Again, he breathed a sigh of relief, as the boat began to set sail.

Ra Heru Khuti began to sense something was wrong because the boat stopped a few feet away from the anchor. He looked over the deck and saw Sethe and one of his agents waving a badge franticly at the gate attendant who still refused to open the gate. Suddenly, Apep reached out and grabbed the attendant by the throat, lifting him off his feet. He continued to assault him as Sethe was going through his pockets for the keys. A shot was heard and the gate attendant collapsed lifelessly to the ground. Two secret agents were still kicking at the gate when the boat again revved its engines and took off. Ra Heru Khuti gazed down at Sethe, Apep and agents waving their badges in the air to get the captain's attention. In a moment of triumph Ra Heru Khuti reached into his coat and pulled out the *Papyrus Am Tuat*. He was certain they could not get aboard. The boat had pulled out far enough away from the dock to make him safe.

Ra Heru Khuti held the manuscript high up in the air and yelled out to Sethe, "You thieves will never own it!" The rest of the passengers looked out with curious faces.

"It is mine! It belongs to me!" Sethe yelled back, fearing Ra Heru Khuti might drop it in the water.

"This is the history of my people! You will never corrupt this!" Sethe and his agents had reached the end of the pier. "You will die! I promise you!" He yelled out.

"No!" Ra Heru Khuti replied, "I live! You will never understand what this is about. These words are not for the dead but the living!" Then he felt the bullet bite into his thigh as his legs buckled under him and brought him to his knees. Blood flowed out of his thigh. The bullet missed his carotid artery by inches. He saw Satra Maat pushing her way past the crowd that gathered around the deck. He still defiantly held the manuscript high in his hands.

"These are sacred words!" he continued to yell at Sethe as the second bullet grazed his shoulders. Satra Maat was at his side trying to shield him from the hale of bullets coming at them.

"Help! Someone, help!" Satra Maat pleaded. But everyone was ducking and running out of the way as bullets hit the deck. Ra Heru Khuti sank into Satraa Maat's arms. They could hear the sirens of the Coast Guard boats as they gave chase.

Suddenly, a familiar face appeared out of the crowd. It was Shekhem Kesnu Neter. Ra Heru Khuti reached out his hands to give him the manuscript which was covered in his blood. "Don't let Sethe get this!" he begged the Shekhem.

Shekhem Kesnu Neter refused to take it. "You take care of it. Your job is not done!" the Shekhem told him as he assisted him to his feet. Suddenly, the Shekhem stopped, staggered and held the railing of the deck. In a moment he collapsed to the floor holding his chest. Blood gushed out of his chest. Sethe's henchman, Apep, who gave chase in one of the Coast Guard boats, gored Shekhem's chest with his evil spear of doom.

Ra Heru Khuti saw the tip of the spear protruding from Shekhem's chest. It entered through the Shekhem's back and came out of his chest. He crawled over to his prostrated body, took the book and placed it on the Shekhem's body. Still, the Shekhem refused to take the book and he told Ra Heru Khuti, "This is not my book! This scroll is yours. The *Papyrus Am Tuat* is the book of your life." Shekhem Kesnu Neter instructed Ra Heru Khuti, "Go to Men Nefer and find Kheper Aunghkti! He will help you!"

Ra Heru Khuti gazed down on the Shekhem's body and rage instantly rose in him.

The Shekhem saw his rage and warned him, "You cannot defeat Sethe with anger in your heart."

"What do you mean?" Ra Heru Khuti asked.

"Anger is Sethe's weapon. To defeat him you have to go within! Now that you have the book of your life you are ready to awaken the warrior within," the Shekhem answered.

"Go within?" Ra Heru Khuti asked.

"It is the warrior within you that will defeat him!" the Shekhem whispered to him.

Meanwhile Apep who had gotten closer to the boat grabbed and tugged the Shekhem's body out of the boat and dragged it to the shore.

Satraa Maat chanted to strengthen Ra Heru Khuti and to give him the power to overcome Sethe and Apep. Blood was gushing out of Ra Heru Khuti's leg. He looked back over the deck to the shoreline and saw Sethe, Apep and the agents surrounding the Shekhem's body like bloodthirsty hyenas moving in for the kill on an injured lion.

Apep stood over the Shekhem's bloody and battered body, steaming with rage. In moments of uncontrolled rage, Apep, the evil one who became incarnate in many forms, especially in wild and savage animals and in monster serpents and venomous reptiles of every kind, slew another follower of Ausar, Shekhem Kesnu Neter. He cried out in awful imprecations and promised terrible destruction to Ra Heru Khuti and his followers, known as the Shemsu Heru. He attacked the Shekhem's torn body by stabbing him repeatedly with the spear. In rage, Apep lifted him and threw him down onto the ground and pinned him under his feet; for this was the moment Apep had been waiting for.

Each day Apep envisioned himself swallowing Ra Heru Khuti's last breath, yet this was the closest he had come to realizing that image. Now, as Apep stood over the Shekhem's body, he was accompanied by his fellow devils and fiends. Apep, bloodied from the carnage looked like he was painted in red and black for he was the deadliest foe of all order, both physical and moral, and of all good in heaven and in Earth.

The Shekhem, in defiance of all the pain he was suffering, weakly held the spear stuck in his chest while lifting the other hand into the air as he vowed to destroy Sethe and Apep who laughed at him.

Ra Heru Khuti saw the Shekhem absorbing the blows from the evil monster Apep. But the Shekhem would not die. His weak voice could still be heard despite Apep's angry screams.

"Lord of the Horizon!" Shekhem Kesnu Neter yelled out, "Make ready a place for me. I come to you as the great face bull! I come to my father Ausar. Anuk Ausar!" The Shekhem's triumphant prayer infuriated Apep who continued to drag Shekhem's body over the rocks on the beach.

Suddenly, Ra Heru Khuti stood up and cast off his human form. Satraa Maat fell away from him for he had changed himself once more into the invincible *Heru Behutet* with his two vultures *Uatchet* and *Nekhebet* at his side. *Heru Behutet* illuminated the sky like two horizons. Electrical outlets all over the city began sparking as they were overcharged with electricity. The city became one brilliant beam of light.

Sethe quickly beckoned to Apep to leave the body and run— for this form of Ra Heru Khuti could not be challenged by men or beast. Both Sethe and Apep, the great enemies of Ausar fled the scene and ran to hide inside an abandoned building. But *Heru Behutet* shot a bolt of fire that paralyzed the monster Apep. *Heru Behutet* continued to advance, shooting more fiery darts into Apep. The monster's body shriveled up under the burning rays of *Heru Behutet's* power, and legions of devils and fiends of darkness from within Apep fled shrieking in terror at their leader's fate.

Then the sun rose. Sethe's fear grew and he withdrew deeper into the underground basement. He soon realized he had trapped himself in a basement with no exit except through the door where *Heru Behutet* stood guard. Both *Uatchet* and *Nekhebet* advised

Heru Behutet not to pursue Sethe but to seal the basement door shut so that he would never again come forth.

"He can do no harm!" they urged *Heru Behutet*, "Seal the door with your fire and let justice back into the world!" *Uatchet* and *Nekhebet* warned Ra Heru Khuti that he had to focus on channeling his energy and powers to connect with his honorable ancestors - the Ashemu - who keep the world in balance, instead of connecting with the Sethians who rule with emotion and keep the world in chaos.

But *Heru Behutet* stood on top of the door that led underground to the basement where Sethe coiled hidden with fear for his transgressions in misleading the children of man. *Heru Behutet* then made the basement a place that burned day and night until the end of days. The underground basement became Sethe's prison – a place where he could no longer observe the stars but only the fire that consumed his endless guilt and shame.

Glossary[25]

Amen: The word the Kamau used to denote the imperceptible aspect of man's (and God's) being. It is the original and essential state of being.

Anetch Hrak: Kamitic greeting or salutation of power directed to those in authority.

Anu: Anu was also known as Heliopolis and On where the Ra philosophy was developed.

Anuk Ausar: translates to "I am Ausar," or one with all.

Ap: The original and unchanging symbol of evil.

Apep: Apep, Nak and Sebau represent the dark forces of the subconscious and symbols of evil. **Apep**: A symbol of evil represented by the serpent.

Apuat: The opener of the way.

Ashemu: A group of priest and priestesses in Khamit developed through the fifth Dynasty.

Ausar: The Kamau (Ancient Egyptians) denotes the desire for oneness, peace and security that comes from it, as the Neter, Ausar.

Bambalasam: One of the ancient Kamitian city buried under the sands of the Sahara.

Behutet: Also known as Herukhuti. Represents the final victory over negative conditionings and thoughts that interfere with realizing one's divinity.

Dark Deceased: An unenlightened deceased person.

Edfu: The main shrine of Heru, the patron God of kingship was located in the city of Edfu.

Herukhuti: The divine principle that safeguards our existence from the injustices of others.

---

[25] For a more detailed explanation and history of most of these terms see: Ra Un Nefer Amen. 1990. *Metu Neter Vol. 1: The Great Oracle of Tehuti and the Egyptian System of Spiritual Cultivation.* (Bronx: Khamit Corp.).

Het Heru: Literally means "House of Heru." The Kamitic principle that expresses itself through inner peace, joy, pleasure, sociability and the positive use of the imagination.

Het Neter: "House of God" or place of worship.

I Ching: A Divination system that has sixty-four hexagrams which represent all the possible situations or mutations of creation.

Khamit/Kamit: Ancient Egypt.

Kush: Means "from the south." People from Kush were called the Kushites.

Maa Kheru: Means "to be justified." You are said to be justified - Maa Kheru - once you complete the Maat initiation system which requires the living of truth.

Maat: Represents the principle of justice and the ideal law.

Men Nefer: Greeks called it Memphis. Men Nefer was the dividing line between Upper and Lower Kamit.

Mesu Betshet: Follower of Sethe.

Metu Neter: One of the primary Oracle systems of Kamit.

Nekhebet: The Goddess Nekhebet, the vulture that protected the Upper part of ancient Egypt, corresponds to the electronegative northern pole and denotes cool psychic and subliminal power.

Papyrus Am Tuat: An initiation system produced by the priest kings of the fifth Dynasty.

Phat: Purification hekau or word of power.

Punt: The homeland of the Egyptians was in Somalia and was called Punt.

Ra: Aroused life-force. It is the active state of the undifferentiated infinite energy/matter from whence all things, living and non living, originate.

Ser-u: Male elders

Sert-u: Female elders

Sethe: Represents an evil symbol. Taken from Kamitic Cosmology where Set is a symbol of confusion and was worshipped by the Hyksos in the most demoniac form.

Shekhem: Power to lead.

Shekhem Ur Shekhem: Translates to "Power, Great Power."

Shemsu Heru: The patrilineal Shemsu Heru (followers of Heru) were the victors of the contest and power struggle between Tawi, the two lands or the twin lands.

Ta Neter: "Ta" means land and "Neter" means God. Ta Neter means the Land of the Gods, or the Divine Land.

Uas Scepter: This is a symbol of well being, happiness and good health.

Uatchet: The Goddess Uatchet protected the Lower part of ancient Egypt. She is symbolized by a venomous cobra, corresponds to the electropositive southern pole and denotes the hot psychic and subliminal power.

Index

Read more about Kazembe at kazembebediako.com.
Or better yet, be his friend on
Facebook.com/kazembebediako
or follow Kazembe on Twitter at
Twitter.com/kazembebediako.

To Order
Please go to:
KazembeBediako.com
Discount rates are available on the website.

Khianga Publishing